THE MARRIAGE
COMMAND

THE MARRIAGE COMMAND

BY

SUSAN FOX

MILLS & BOON®

First published in Great Britain 2003
Large Print edition 2004
Harlequin Mills & Boon Limited,
Eton House, 18-24 Paradise Road,
Richmond, Surrey TW9 1SR

© Susan Fox 2003

ISBN 0 263 18057 3

Set in Times Roman 17 on 19 pt.
16-0304-43819

Printed and bound in Great Britain
by Antony Rowe Ltd, Chippenham, Wiltshire

CHAPTER ONE

CLAIRE RYAN'S first contact with Logan Pierce had been six months ago at her stepsister's funeral. Because Farrah had alienated most people and had few friends left, the sad little service had been only minimally attended. The forty or so people who'd shown up had mostly been Claire's friends, and they'd attended out of respect for her rather than Farrah.

The only person Claire hadn't recognized had been the tall, rugged stranger in the coal black suit and dress Stetson who'd walked in looking harsh and unapproachable. The moment Claire had caught sight of him, her attention had been seized by the wild impression that he was some sort of human manifestation of death itself.

5

If she'd known then who he was and why he'd come to Farrah's funeral, she would have fled the chapel and raced home to snatch up little Cody and disappear. But the singular drawback of having a modest, stable life was that it had been impossible to just pack up and run, not even to keep Farrah's eighteen-month-old son.

Because she hadn't been able to run all those weeks and months ago—as much because of her sense of honor as her settled situation—Claire was about to lose the one person she loved with all her heart.

It had taken every scrap of integrity she'd had to force herself to obey the court's order and drive all the way from San Antonio to the Pierce Ranch that afternoon. She'd slowed her older model car to a crawl as she'd approached the huge single-story ranch house at the headquarters of what had to be one of the largest ranches in that part of Texas.

She'd parked at the end of the front walk, then got out to gather the sleepy two-year-old from his car seat to carry him to the door. The housekeeper, who'd introduced herself as Elsa, had opened the door for her immediately, then got her and little Cody seated in the living room before she briskly went to the kitchen to bring back a tray of iced tea and orange juice that she'd set on the coffee table. After taking a few silent moments to pour a glass of tea and a smaller one of juice, the woman had disappeared into another part of the big house.

Claire felt her throat spasm more tightly closed as she ignored the tea and cuddled the drowsy boy against herself. Emotion that was the most poignant and painful of her life made her eyes sting yet again.

After today, or after tomorrow at the latest, she might never see this precious little boy again. Legally, she no longer had even a small claim to him, though morally she was far more entitled to be his mother than Farrah had been.

It had been Claire who'd taken care of the boy from the day he'd come home from the hospital. Claire who'd gotten up with him in the night, Claire who'd fed him, bathed him, taken him for checkups, played with him. And Claire who had paid for anything and everything the child had needed. And though it had been Claire who'd loved him more than her life, none of that had counted for anything with the judge.

Farrah hadn't bonded at all with the child and she certainly hadn't wanted the responsibility of raising him. The truth was, she'd only kept the unplanned and unwanted pregnancy in hopes of getting her rich former boyfriend to marry her. Or failing that—and she had failed to wrangle a marriage proposal out of the father—she'd meant to extort some lavish amount of child support from him. But then Cliff Pierce had been killed before Cody had been born.

That was all Claire had known. The day after Cody's birth, Farrah had brought the infant directly to her, then promptly gone to live with one of the few friends she hadn't yet alienated.

The moment Claire had taken the tiny infant into her arms, she'd fallen instantly and irrevocably in love. She'd understood right away that her flighty stepsister meant for the arrangement to be permanent, but she hadn't been able to persuade Farrah to make her the baby's legal guardian.

Claire had recognized Farrah's refusal for what it was: an opportunity to maintain legal control over the child in case a future opportunity presented itself.

And it had presented itself in the form of Cliff Pierce's older brother—his very rich older brother—who was sole heir to all things Pierce.

That's why Logan Pierce had shown up at Farrah's funeral to make contact with Claire. That's why he'd taken her to court to continue the process of claiming his late brother's only child. Farrah hadn't informed Claire that she'd already petitioned the courts for child support from Cody's uncle, so finding out about it after Farrah's sudden death had been a shock.

Cliff Pierce had taken a blood test before Cody's birth, and once Cody was born, his blood had also been tested, so there was no doubt of paternity. Then a week ago, the court had deemed Logan Pierce more entitled and qualified to raise little Cody than she was.

A stepaunt's rights—though she'd virtually been a mother to the child—had been trumped in the courts by the rights of blood kin. If she'd had the money to continue to fight for access to the boy, she might at least have had a legal chance. But her money was no match for Pierce resources.

And because Cody's blood kin was too coldhearted to concede her right to anything to do with the boy, today was the beginning of the end. Her last obligation was to hand Cody over. But would the man who was so determined to have his nephew all to himself allow her to at least help the child through what would surely be a traumatic transition?

She would find some way to survive the loss of the boy, but Cody was far too young to make sense of any of this. All he would understand was that the woman he thought of as his mother had suddenly abandoned him. Why the judge hadn't been able to understand that worried her less than Logan Pierce's apparent indifference to the emotional consequences of separation for little Cody.

The temptation to throw herself at Logan Pierce's feet and beg to be allowed at least a miniscule part in the boy's future was pitifully strong. If she could somehow keep the child from being devastated, she was willing to do whatever it took to spare him.

And yet she knew instinctively that she couldn't show even a particle of emotion. A

Claire "Momma." Though Claire had worried about that from the start, she had been Cody's momma in every way other than actually giving birth to him. The tragedy for her, but now especially for the boy, was that she hadn't.

As if he'd sensed her upset, Cody moved restlessly in her arms and drew back to rub his eye with a back of his hand. His soft whimper was a strong signal that he was out of sorts. He'd not slept well in the car, and the lack of a good nap would leave him cranky until he felt more fully awake. This wasn't the best time for him to meet his uncle.

The housekeeper had offered no real welcome to the boy, though most people did. Cody was a handsome child, with black hair and blue eyes, and he was usually well behaved. It helped to remember that he'd had his little arms fastened tightly around Claire's neck when they'd come in, so perhaps the housekeeper hadn't thought he was awake enough yet to cope with a stranger.

Claire so hoped that was the reason the woman had all but ignored the boy. At least she'd brought a carafe of cold orange juice with the pitcher of iced tea, so perhaps that was an indication of the woman's thoughtfulness.

Cody began to fuss a little then, and Claire tried to distract him.

''Would you like some orange juice, sweetheart?''

That got his attention and she scooted forward on the sofa with him on her lap to reach for the small glass. Cody seemed to perk up a bit after he'd had a sip, but he refused a second sip. He'd noticed a small bronze sculpture of a wild horse on the table at the end of the sofa and immediately wiggled out of her arms to investigate.

And promptly knocked the small, weighty piece on its side!

Horrified, Claire put the glass of juice on the tray then jumped up to right the sculpture. The moment she picked it up, she saw that the rippling mane of the horse had gouged the fine, high gloss tabletop. The whitish cut stood out starkly on the dark wood.

How would Logan Pierce react to this? The question made her nauseous, and her heart began to race with real fear. But then her fear shot up what must have been miles as she heard heavy bootsteps coming from some unseen hall outside the wide doorway of the living room.

There was no way to fix or conceal the damage to what was surely a very expensive table. She would gladly pay for the damage whatever it cost, but a two-year-old was bound to have other small accidents in a home filled with fine furniture, and she wouldn't be around to intervene with those.

As the steady bootsteps grew closer, she sent up a desperate prayer.

Please, God, let him be tenderhearted with this boy. And understanding and wonderfully patient…

That was the moment Logan Pierce walked into the room. Claire looked up from the damaged table and tried to read his somber expression as she clutched the small sculpture.

There was nothing even remotely tender or understanding or patient about the way this man looked. His rugged face was all planes and angles and harshness. He looked almost ruthless. She doubted he'd ever smiled in his life.

And then he leveled that cold black gaze on her and she felt the sharp impact of it. She could tell he didn't like her—that had been obvious from the moment she'd seen him at the funeral—but her worries about his bad opinion of her were a distant second to her fear that Cody's accident just now might cause him to have a bad opinion of the boy.

Pierce was clearly not a m n to cross or aggravate or inconvenienc in any way, which made him the last p on Claire would pick to raise her beloved Cody. Jus e fact that he'd deemed her unimportant t hild was enough to convince her t at he ldn't care about Cody's feelings in any r cir- cumstances. Particularly furniture gouges.

That hard black gaze dropped to note the bronze horse she still held in her hands. He hadn't greeted her, not even to make a token welcome, so she didn't offer one, though she was compelled to speak.

"There's been a small accident, Mr. Pierce. I'm afraid your table has been dam- aged, and I apologize for not being quick enough to prevent it. If you'll send me the bill, I'll gladly pay for either a repair or a replacement, whichever you prefer."

Claire held her breath, so terrified of how he'd react that she felt almost faint. Cody's voice carried a cranky whine.

"I want the horse, Momma."

Claire glanced down at him, relieved to be spared a few seconds of the intensity in Logan Pierce's gaze. She set the sculpture on the coffee table next to the tray.

"The horse isn't a toy, honey," she said softly as she took the boy's hand to redirect his attention. "You need to say hello to your uncle." She gave the child an encouraging smile.

Cody glanced over his shoulder to see the giant of a man who stood a few feet away, then promptly turned back to Claire and launched himself against her. Claire picked him up and his little arms went tightly around her neck. There was no mistaking his fear, and Logan's disapproval was evident.

"Does he act up like that all the time?"

The question was a criticism of the boy that was almost impossible to tolerate, though she managed to do it.

"He's very well behaved, Mr. Pierce. He didn't get a good nap on the way out, so he's out of sorts. And this is a new place. He's shy with people he doesn't know, and I'm glad of that. I hope you'll be patient. He's really a very good little boy. Very good.''

She took a shaky breath, compelled to win some sign of softening on Pierce's harsh face. ''He's only two years old.''

Her voice broke on the words so she went silent and tried not to look as terrified for Cody—and as worried about Logan Pierce's obvious displeasure—as she felt.

''Why are you glad?''

The odd question threw her for a moment, but he helpfully supplied a reminder.

''You said he's shy with people he doesn't know. Why are you glad?''

Claire sensed more than a trace of anger behind the question, as if he'd taken her remarks personally.

''I'm sure you read the papers and listen to the news, Mr. Pierce. A child who's too friendly with strangers is at risk, so yes, I'm glad he's leery of strangers. I'm sure he'll be fine once he gets to know you. Please don't be offended.''

The heavy silence that descended was rife with undercurrents. As intimidating as Logan Pierce was, Claire couldn't seem to keep from staring.

The man wasn't handsome, at least not in the conventional way. His weathered tan gave the impression of Native ancestry that went with his almost black hair and midnight eyes. And yet it was his very ruggedness that would make him a standout anywhere he went.

He was tall and wide-shouldered, with strong arms and long, powerful legs. He obviously spent the bulk of his time outdoors doing hard physical labor, and the blue plaid shirt he wore with the cuffs folded back, his jeans and scuffed black boots were clearly work clothes.

The overall impression was raw masculinity unrelieved by any trace of softness. Claire knew already that he was a tyrant who was used to getting his way, either by the sheer overpowering force of his will or by buying it. He'd used both to stake his claim to Cody and he'd been soundly successful.

But did he have it in him to extend some small particle of mercy to the woman he'd so decisively trounced in court? Claire would gladly forego any possible concession to her in exchange for his pledge to be gentle and understanding with the boy.

Cody's whispered, ''Wanna go home, Mommy,'' wasn't quite enough of a whisper.

If it was possible, Logan Pierce's harsh expression went harsher. Claire sensed right away that he blamed her for the boy's eagerness to leave. She broke contact with his cold gaze to speak with the child.

''We came to visit your uncle Logan, sweetheart. Remember? We brought your toys so you'd have plenty to play with in case your uncle didn't have many toys.''

Claire persuaded the boy to loosen his hold on her neck so he could see her face. She made herself smile. ''Maybe we can have Uncle Logan help us bring in a few things. Would you like that? I'm sure he'd like to see your cars.''

''No, Momma,'' Cody said, his little face the picture of distress before he cuddled close again. ''I wanna go home,'' he said, then burst into tears.

The sound wounded her and she looked over at Logan. ''Do you have a rocking chair?'' If she could get Cody to settle down enough to finish his nap, it would make all the difference.

Logan didn't reply to that, but instead turned to walk to the wide doorway he'd entered the room by moments ago. He obviously expected her to follow, so she gathered up her handbag and the large cloth bag of Cody's things. She awkwardly balanced her hold on the sobbing child with one arm as she swung the long straps of both bags over her shoulder and started around the long sofa.

When she got to the hall, she turned in the direction Logan had gone. She passed the open double doors to a formal dining room before she reached a second long hall to the left that apparently led to the bedroom end of the large house. Claire hadn't realized that the house was laid out in an L-shape. Somehow she'd not noticed it, possibly because the ranch driveway had brought her directly toward the house and she'd been too upset over finally arriving to pay attention.

Her ungracious host was waiting outside the door of a bedroom and she ignored his deepening frown when his dark gaze dropped to note the large bag that no doubt looked as heavy and cumbersome as it felt.

A gentleman would have offered to carry it for her, but because he might not have seen it sitting on the floor during his brief visit to the living room, he'd not had an opportunity to be helpful.

On the other hand, the rude way he'd walked out of the living room to lead the way here, easily outdistancing her and the sobbing boy as if they were both too disruptive to tolerate, made her conclude that chivalrous acts—if he even knew what those were— weren't automatically conferred on those he deemed unworthy of them.

And this was the creature who would raise Cody.

Claire turned carefully with her burdens to walk through the doorway, and the sight of the bedroom made her heart fall. It was a child's room, a little boy's, and it had obviously been decorated by a professional. It was another hurtful reminder that Cody's place was here now, and not with her. Everything, from the wallpaper to the drapes to the beds—and there were two of those— had been beautifully coordinated.

A variety of charming baby animals made up the wallpaper design that covered the walls above the glossy wood wainscoting, and were picked up again by a couple of lamps on the dresser and chest of drawers.

The baby animals were repeated on the coverlets of both beds. A huge wooden rocking horse that looked as if it had been hand-crafted generations ago sat in a corner.

A gigantic toy box with a safety-hinged lid stood open in another corner, but the area in front of low triple windows featured a miniature wood table and four little chairs. Two bookcases were half-filled with books that looked so new they might have been bought in a bookstore that day.

One of the two beds was a baby bed, but the other was a single bed with a solid wood headboard. Claire guessed right away that the tall silent man who'd followed her into the room had decreed the choice of both. First because he didn't know which bed size was appropriate for the boy's age and wouldn't humble himself enough to ask, and second because he was a man with too much money to worry about an unnecessary cost.

Unless he'd figured the baby bed, if not needed, could be used by a future son or daughter of his own. Claire didn't know much about Logan Pierce but she did know he was single, though after her unpleasant encounters with him, it was her opinion that the baby bed would go to waste. She couldn't imagine that any principled woman would be willing to marry such a cold-blooded man and allow him to father her children, not even to have access to his fortune.

Claire carried Cody directly to the rocking chair that sat between the baby bed and the regular bed. She took a moment to pull a diaper out of the cloth bag before she let the shoulder straps to both her bags slide down her arm to the floor and turned with the boy to the baby bed.

With the ease of long practice, she managed to hold the boy and the diaper while she lowered the side of the bed. She laid him on the quilt-covered mattress then unhooked the boy's little overalls to change him. The moment she got him fastened back up, she lifted Cody and carried him to the private bathroom that had also been expertly decorated. She disposed of the diaper, then set the fussy child on the counter next to the sink while she washed her hands.

When she finished and carried the boy out to the rocking chair, Logan Pierce hadn't moved an inch from where he stood, watching everything. Claire ignored him and sat down with the tired little boy who was still fretting.

Claire had never been rattled by Cody's crying or fussiness before, but today it put her on edge. The utter silence from Logan Pierce warned her he wasn't taking this well, and Claire worried that Cody's potential to have a good relationship with his uncle was being damaged a little more every moment he acted less than the perfect child.

Thank God there was no nanny evident, so Logan couldn't send her away too quickly unless he wanted to manage Cody on his own.

The rocking chair was a fine one, and it moved smoothly. Claire kept her attention on the boy or on the wall or on the windows as she rocked and patiently soothed the boy by rubbing his back. He wound down fairly quick and after a few minutes he was resting heavily against her.

What would happen once she put him in the baby bed? Would Logan show her the door? Since she had no legal rights over the boy, she and Cody were literally at the mercy of a man who didn't appear to know the meaning of the word.

But surely, *surely* the man knew it was a bad idea to banish her and let the boy wake up later without a chance to even say good-bye.

Claire pressed a desperate kiss to the boy's forehead and felt again the stark pain of impending loss. Her heart was about to be torn out, but it was the boy who would bleed. How would he ever understand? How would he ever get over the trauma of being suddenly abandoned by her?

Logan's gravely drawl pushed at her.

''He's asleep.''

The message was clear. *The boy's asleep, so put him in bed.* Dread made her brain add the words, Don't let the door hit your backside on the way out...

Claire almost couldn't force herself to stop rocking and stand. The seconds fell heavily, one by one, impacting her heart like sharp spears as she carried the soundly sleeping two-year-old to the baby bed and carefully laid him on his side atop the plush little quilt.

Unable to step away too quickly, unable to keep from taking what might be a last opportunity, she leaned down and kissed the boy's satiny cheek. The wetness that blurred everything was almost impossible to hold back but she did. And then she straightened and quietly eased the side of the bed up until it locked into place.

She didn't look at the big man who loomed at arm's length as she stepped away to gather up her purse and the cloth bag. The bag would stay with the boy, but she needed to show Logan some of the things she'd packed in it.

Cody's vitamins and his baby book were included in the contents, along with a detailed printout of everything to do with his health, from vaccinations to doctor's names and the schedule of future appointments for check-ups.

She'd even photocopied the meticulous little diary she'd kept, but that, along with a baby book containing photos and keepsakes identical to the one she'd made for Logan Pierce, would stay with her forever.

Claire carried her things to the door, taking a few seconds to pause and glance back at the sleeping boy before she reached the hall. Because Logan had followed her and his big body blocked her view, she leaned to the side for a last glimpse.

Cody was lying asleep just as she'd left him, so there was no excuse to linger. She turned and went on out the door into the hall and started back the way she'd come on legs that felt heavy and weak. They reached the wide doorway to the living room before she stopped and turned back to Logan.

''Will you check on him regularly? It will upset him to wake up in a strange place.'' She hesitated, wanting badly to add the words *without me,* but instead added, ''Alone.''

Logan tilted his head back the tiniest bit as he stared down at her. Claire felt the cut of his dark gaze and quailed a little inside. The man was stern, and as unmoved as a column of stone. She'd never felt so powerless against anyone or anything in her life before this man had crossed her path. He was taking everything that mattered to her and she almost couldn't bear the roaring frustration of being unable to prevent it or to even slow him down.

Claire had never hated anyone in her entire life, but she was close to hating this man. And if he harmed so much as a hair on that sweet boy or failed to love him wholeheartedly or unconditionally, or abused him, she'd somehow find out about it. And when she did, she'd also find the means, some way or somehow, to destroy Logan Pierce.

"Are you so eager to dump him off and get home?"

Logan's low words shocked her and she almost pinched herself to make sure she was actually awake and that something wasn't wrong with her hearing. Or was she just so desperate to be able to stay as long as he'd tolerate that she was having a delusion?

Claire couldn't answer the question at first, but when she registered the challenge to her devotion, she felt a flash of anger.

"I'm not eager to leave him anywhere, Mr. Pierce."

"Especially not with me," he added as smoothly as if he'd read her mind. Claire's gaze fell from contact with his.

"I'm…worried for him. You clearly expect me to just leave him here and not come back. Do you realize how traumatic that will be for him?"

Now she looked up at him, unable to keep the rest from boiling out.

"He's not a week old or a month old. He's a trusting little boy who's lived his whole life with a woman he thinks of as his mother. Do you have any idea how devastating it will be for him if I'm forced to leave him here forever, with a man he's never met before today?"

That was the moment Logan reached for her arm. She flinched and tried to draw back, but he caught her elbow and she nearly jumped out of her skin. The bolt of electricity that went through her from his steely fingers sent a heavy wave of weakness through her.

''We'll finish this in private,'' he growled, and before she could react, he was ushering her on past the living room then down the long hall that paralleled the front of the house. The power in his grip, though it was amazingly gentle, was a silent manifestation of male strength.

Whatever he'd just said about finishing this in private, Claire was terrified that he was about to throw her out of his house.

CHAPTER TWO

THEY'D almost reached the hall entrance into the front foyer before Claire found her tongue.

"Please, Mr. Pierce, I don't care what you do to me, but please think of the boy."

She felt his big body go taut, as if his muscles were bunching in preparation to inflict violence. She was almost too dizzy with dread to register that they'd passed the entry hall and were truly on their way to some other destination besides the front door.

The large book-lined room he led her into was obviously a den or office. He paused, his grip on her arm pulling her to a halt too while he shoved the door solidly closed behind them. Only then did he release her.

"Pick a place to sit," he told her gruffly then crossed the room to a huge desk that sat faced away from a set of glass double doors to the patio beyond. There were two leather wing chairs just this side of the desk, but there were two more at the side of the room on either side of a low table where another tray of iced tea sat. Judging by the lack of heavy condensation on the outside of the crystal pitcher, it must have just been brought in.

Claire stood edgily near the door, relieved to not have been thrown out of the house, but furious that he'd marched her in here like that. She didn't want to "pick a place to sit." Logan didn't look like he planned to sit for at least a week either. They were both wound up and tense, and she was so on guard with him now that she didn't want to go anywhere near him.

She was still tingling from his warm grip, still amazed that the crushing power she'd sensed in his fingers had been restrained to the point of gentleness. As big and strong as he was, his gentle grip was a stunning contrast.

She caught a glimpse of frustration in the way he yanked open a desk drawer and pulled out a thick file of papers. He appeared to be furious, but to his credit he didn't explode, though she could read anger in every line of his body. Seeing that was another confirmation of the contrast between brute strength and gentleness in him, but she didn't dare read so much into so little.

He pushed the drawer closed with a snap then walked to the wing chairs at the side of the room with the file. He shot her a surly glance.

''Are you gonna sit or not?''

Claire saw even more frustration but there was also a glimmer of discomfort, almost regret, in his dark eyes before they went flat and cold again.

Intrigued and marginally encouraged by that humanizing hint of discomfort, she walked over to the wing chair opposite the one he stood next to. She took the straps of both bags off her shoulder then sat down and placed them on the floor at her feet. That seemed to mollify him somewhat so he sat down.

The twin to the large leather wing chair she sat in looked too small for the big man, and she was again impressed by his size and obvious physical power. Cody had mostly been around women. The few men he'd had contact with were smaller in stature than Logan Pierce and more...well, civilized looking. Perhaps this explained why Cody's first glimpse of his towering uncle had startled and upset him, and Claire began to worry about that too.

Though helping Cody adjust favorably to his uncle was akin to cutting her own throat, Claire was suddenly just as desperate for the boy to not be afraid of Logan as she was for Logan to genuinely love the boy and treat him kindly.

Her grim host tossed the thick file of paper onto the table between them. Fortunately, the small table could accommodate both the tray and the file.

Ignoring the propriety of offering his guest a glass of iced tea, Logan settled back in his chair and his dark gaze again cut over her face.

''That's everything I have on you,'' he growled, meaning the file, before he started detailing a list. ''Honest, hardworking, long-suffering and patient with fools and promiscuous stepsisters, never been in trouble, churchgoing, self-employed from the week after the boy was born, and as chaste with men and as saintly with abandoned babies as a Mother Theresa. It's a damned wonder you weren't quite perfect enough to find a lawyer with enough smarts to get a file like this in front of the judge.''

Claire sat, wide-eyed and frozen in breathless shock at the litany of attributes he seemed to resent mightily, while they also managed to be a litany of backhanded and grudging compliments. Plus, he was all but declaring that she'd been victimized by an incompetent and ineffectual lawyer.

Did he feel guilty about steamrolling her in court? Perhaps, but it was clear that he resented feeling that guilt. Or was this a sign that he hadn't truly wanted to win so much? Had he changed his mind about taking on the challenge and responsibility of raising his late brother's orphaned son all by himself? Claire waited a moment more, both to somehow think of something to say as to give him an opportunity to go on speaking if he was going to.

''I'm not sure I understand what you're getting at, Mr. Pierce, and I have no idea why you seem to be angry,'' she began calmly when he hadn't said anything more. ''You got everything you asked for in court, while I got seven days after the judge's ruling to bring Cody out here and turn him over to you.''

The surly line of his dark brow nettled her into adding softly, ''If anyone's entitled to be rude and cold and resentful, I don't think it's you, sir.''

She saw the glittering flare that shot through his dark eyes before he controlled it. The stern line of his mouth appeared to relax the tiniest bit.

''How bad do you want to keep the boy?''

Claire's heart leaped with hope. Was he serious? Otherwise, it was a cruel question if he was merely bating her to draw her out so he could somehow use her answer to hurt her. On the other hand, what if he was asking because he wanted to confirm something for himself before he made some sort of offer that would give her at least minimal contact with Cody after today?

Oh God, she didn't dare trust him. She was devastated enough over the impending loss of the boy. Claire thought about it a moment longer then decided she might as well answer his question. What did she have left of any value aside from whatever time—probably no more than minutes or, at best, hours—that she might yet get to have with Cody? Nothing else mattered to her but him, not even her pride, and without Cody there was nothing more anyone could ever take from her or hurt her with.

''Did your investigator write in that file that I love Cody just as fiercely as if he were my own little boy?'' she started evenly. ''That the very best moments in my life are when he's smiling and happy, or when he discovers something new or when he learns how to do something he wasn't able to do before? Is it written anywhere in your file, Mr. Pierce, that I'd lay my life down for him without a second thought? Or that I'd kill to protect him?''

How she managed to say all that while holding back an ever-rising tide of strangling tears, she didn't know. She lifted her chin the slightest fraction and finished.

"Did your investigator print a warning page in there somewhere? Something that might read, 'Caution. Don't ever mistreat the boy, or this chaste, long-suffering, church-going, Mother Theresa clone might come after you with mayhem in mind?' That's how much I love the boy, Mr. Pierce. So yes, I'd probably do just about anything to keep him if I had no respect or regard for the law.''

The moment she finished speaking the words, Claire felt sick. What had she been thinking? She needed whatever goodwill this man might be able to stir up. The fact was that she'd been distraught for months now over the impending loss of Cody. This past week had been sheer hell, and suddenly all her rigid control was crumbling. Her heart was screaming with desperation and vicious pain. Somehow she managed to get the words past her tight throat.

"I apologize, Mr. Pierce. I'm very upset. Beyond upset. I'm a little frantic about how Cody will survive all this when he doesn't know you at all. He's just a little boy, such a sweet little boy..."

Claire's breaking voice made her stop, and it was a good thing. No sense further damaging things between them by showing even more emotion or by threatening Logan Pierce any more than she already had.

That cold black gaze probed hers and then cut over her as deliberately as if he was dicing a vegetable.

Oh God, she really had blown it. Blown it completely. Surely he would immediately usher her out the front door and drag her to her car. After her threat of mayhem, he might even have someone follow her all the way to the highway and probably to the county line.

The stupidity of losing control could come at such a heavy price that she might not survive the paying of it. She'd not been sure she could live with the loss of Cody, but if any chance to see him again had just been ruined by what she'd said—something *she'd* done this time—Claire didn't know how she'd be able to live with herself.

"I've behaved badly, but I've apologized, sincerely apologized, Mr. Pierce. I hope you'll understand that this is a very emotional time."

There was absolutely no flicker of change in those awful black eyes or even a faint hint of softening on his stony features.

Claire couldn't imagine how Cody could begin to deal with this man! She was utterly intimidated, but Cody would be terrified. What on earth could she do to protect him? She wasn't even certain she could protect herself.

Her brain was racing so frantically that she didn't catch what Logan said to her then.

"Pardon me?" Her voice was barely a squeak now and it was all she could do to keep from crying. Her head was so full of tears that her ears were roaring.

"I asked why you're twenty-four and not married."

The out-of-the-blue question was a new shock, and she answered before she thought about it. "I'm not sure that's any of your business. Just as it's not my place to ask you why you're not married."

Again she saw the glittering flare in his dark eyes, and realized with some surprise that what she was seeing was male interest. She almost wished it had been a signal of anger. That she would understand. But interest? She had to be misreading him. He was probably furious, though his stony expression made it difficult to detect anything more certain than harshness.

"Then you need to know that I just made it my business, Miss Ryan," he said gruffly, emphasizing the formal use of her name the same way she'd emphasized the formal use of his by addressing him as Mr. Pierce.

"I want to know if you're capable of being a wife. The boy ought to have more than one parent at a time. Are you capable of being as good a wife as you are a good mother?"

Claire gave her head a small, dazed shake. "I suppose."

"A traditional wife who stays home? One who can run a house, entertain guests, arrange her husband's social life? Spend his money, have good sex, raise his kids?"

He paused, making Claire realize her face probably showed her utter shock. The little shocks he'd dealt her so far that day were nothing compared to this, and suddenly she knew he was on the verge of presenting her with the biggest shock yet.

Claire felt the room tip a little and her head began to swim. She had to be misunderstanding this whole bizarre conversation, *had* to be, so she made a try at another interpretation.

"Are you saying that if I found a husband and was a stay-at-home wife and mother, that you might consider allowing me to raise Cody? If that's the case, then yes, I'm more than capable of being a good wife the moment I find a suitable husband."

Claire realized she was shaking all over suddenly as the roaring in her ears got a little louder. But as loud as that roaring was, it was amazing how clearly she heard what he said next. Though his voice was still a low, gravelly drawl that was almost a growl, it was as loud in her ears and in her brain as if he'd yelled out the words.

"I meant, be a good wife *to me,* Miss Ryan. Marry me. Agree to all the things I mentioned, and I'll allow you to adopt the boy when I adopt him. Otherwise, I'll let you stay here through the weekend, but Monday morning you'll have to leave. The boy and I will have to work things out between us without your help."

I meant, be a good wife to me, *Miss Ryan...*

The room began to spin as those words and those next ones, *Marry me,* began to go round and round in her brain. But then the other things he'd listed before began to rush in a chaotic circle around those.

Run a house, entertain guests, arrange her husband's social life, spend his money, raise his kids...

They weren't bad words, they weren't unpleasant words. In fact, they conjured up the kind of homey, satisfying scenes she'd always longed to see fulfilled when she found the right man and got married.

But then that other little item he'd specified, *good sex,* began to race around with all the others, somehow sparkling and tumbling and very quickly dominating all the other images his list had called up.

Claire tried to focus on the big man, the supremely harsh and powerful looking big man, who sat across from her and had just cold-bloodedly proposed a loveless marriage to a woman he didn't know outside of a private investigator's report. A man who, judging by the unremitting harshness on his stony face, still didn't seem to even like her.

As stunned and overwhelmed as she was, it was the heartless declaration of blackmail that touched off a conflagration of outrage.

Otherwise, I'll let you stay here through the weekend, but Monday morning you'll have to leave. The boy and I will have to work things out between us without your help.

Claire was on her feet without making a conscious decision to stand. It was a poor choice because her legs felt like spaghetti, though sheer temper might carry her through a ten-mile marathon.

"Please indulge me, Mr. Pierce," she began with strained softness, and it was hard not to grit her teeth as she said the words. "Did you say that if I don't agree to marry you, that I'll never see the boy again after Monday?"

He tipped his head back slightly to keep eye contact with her. He looked relaxed, damn him. And she suddenly caught a hint of enjoyment that nettled her even more because there was something indulgent in it. As if he liked women with prickly tempers because he found them entertaining, though he wouldn't for a moment take those tempers seriously. Which was male arrogance at its most aggravating.

''I won't hire you to nanny the boy because it wouldn't set right for him to have a nanny he calls momma,'' he said. ''I don't care to sort through the women I know to find one who'll be as much a mother to him as she will be to kids of her own.''

Then he delivered a rapid-fire list that stoked her outrage higher with each item.

''I like your potential. Dress you up a little, get a little glamour on you, and I'll be satisfied with the package. If you're as good a wife as you are a mother, I'll be satisfied with that, too, and you can adopt the boy.''

Claire was so infuriated by that list, especially his ''get a little glamour on you'' remark, that she could barely keep the red haze out of her vision.

''And if you're not satisfied with 'the package'?'' Oh how she loathed those words!

''You aren't the kind of woman who takes something on if you can't commit yourself to it. And once you're committed, you follow through, whether you made a good bargain or not. Farrah is just one example.''

The harshness on his face had eased into a look of self-satisfaction. He had her pegged, and he had no compunction against letting her know he had. And he held the one thing she wanted with all her heart, so he was confident she'd knuckle under to everything he'd listed.

But if she could find some way to tolerate this arrogant manipulator and bring herself to marry him, she'd become Cody's legal mother. The courts could then be compelled to grant her equal standing in custody issues, should she and Logan divorce.

Claire knew instantly that if she submitted to such heartless blackmail and actually married this—this *creature*—that there *would* be a divorce on the horizon. As soon after she became Cody's legal mother as was humanly possible.

That was the commitment she'd be making if she agreed to marry Logan Pierce.

But oh, *oh* how she'd love to punch that arrogant look off his face! Claire had never had violent feelings before today, she'd never lifted her hand to hurt anyone in her life. But she'd never felt so wildly angry and trapped and frustrated as this man had made her feel when she'd officially lost Cody to him. That had brought her close enough to hating him.

But her anger now and this trapped and frustrated feeling was suddenly so intensely personal that she was bubbling inside. And she was scared out of her mind over the idea of having to submit to anything even remotely sexual with him. She doubted she could even stand to hold his hand, much less kiss him. Never mind the rest.

Good sex, he'd said. At the moment, she couldn't associate either the word ''good'' or the word ''sex'' with Logan Pierce.

Though she was compelled to ask what she did next, Claire knew right away that Logan could tell she wasn't serious about the question, that it was merely a delay. She couldn't associate the word "love" with Logan Pierce any more easily than the words "good" or "sex."

"What about love? You've said nothing about love."

Or respect, but she reckoned that asking him about respect was laughable at this point. Respect for her was something she'd force him to learn one way or another, whether he wanted to master that particular lesson or not.

It was remarkable how quickly his arrogant, self-satisfied look stiffened and went harsh again.

"I don't put stock in love, Miss Ryan. It's not important."

Claire nodded, not surprised. "You don't have any to give, either, is that what you're saying?"

She didn't wait for him to answer that. ''Well, you'll need to scrape up some for Cody. I don't care about love from you, either, but I won't stand for you to not be loving to the boy. I also won't tolerate any kind of abuse from you. No dragging me around like you did earlier, and if you ever raise a hand to Cody or to me, you'll never get a second chance.''

Now his dark brows lowered into surly whorls. ''I've never raised my hand to a woman or a child, and I'll be damned if I'll let you think I would.''

She gave a small nod. ''Good. That's good. I'm very glad to hear that. And I'm sure you've figured out by now that any marriage we might make won't be a one-way street with everything going only your way.''

''Then the answer is yes.''

''The answer is, I'll think about it.''

His dark eyes glittered again and some of that arrogant satisfaction ghosted back over his harsh, unhandsome face. ''Fair enough.''

Claire gave her head a decisive shake. "No it's not fair, Mr. Pierce. None of this is. You might as well know now that I don't think much of you for using the boy to manipulate me like this."

She saw the flare of anger that caused, but the knock that came at the closed door to the hall startled her. Logan called out a terse, "What is it?" that diffused a fraction of the taut tension between them.

Elsa's voice sounded subdued. "The boy's awake."

Concern for Cody waking up so soon distracted Claire, who promptly abandoned her things and hurried to the door to open it and rush through the house to Cody's bedroom. The fact that Logan stayed behind in the den and allowed her to go alone gave her some much needed time to recover from the wild turmoil of raw emotion that tested her more savagely than anything ever had in her life.

What on earth should she do now? What could she do? The anxious questions answered themselves the moment she reached Cody's bedroom and rushed across the room to take the boy in her arms. It seemed to take forever to quit shaking and regain her composure.

CHAPTER THREE

LOGAN had a rare appreciation for fiery women. He hadn't expected the very proper, coolly composed Ms. Ryan to have that spark. Until today, she'd appeared meek and maybe a little too self-sacrificing. She'd seemed almost too much a Polly Pureheart for his personal taste, yet all the qualities he'd seen would do to make a fair, easily managed wife. He'd thought her full potential could be brought out and molded, that he could solve a lot of problems by getting her to marry him.

But then he'd seen that fire and it interested him. The lady had a temper, and she wasn't quite the meek Goody Two-shoes he'd taken her for—the meek Goody Two-shoes he'd felt so guilty for squashing in court, the Goody Two-shoes he'd felt so guilty for taking the kid away from.

But she'd marry him now however angry she was, he was certain of it. And it eased his conscience to find out she wasn't quite the gracious loser he'd thought, though he planned to reward her handsomely for losing to him. She'd be glad to raise the boy and grateful to do it, she'd enjoy having a fine house and all the money she wanted.

Though she probably couldn't tell by how he'd acted today, he knew how to treat a lady like a queen, he knew how to satisfy one in bed.

As long as none of that required him to involve his heart, he could afford to be magnanimous. Besides, now that he'd got custody of Cliff's boy and he was safely under his roof, Logan was ready to have other heirs. It bothered him that he and Cody were the last of the Texas Pierces. The only way to remedy that was to have more kids. Two or three besides Cody would be an impressive start.

The three months of marriage he'd planned to have with Claire before a conception, would ensure that Cody would be the right age by the time another baby arrived. After all, three years between kids seemed to be considerate to the mother. And now that Claire Ryan was here and she'd passed muster, there was no reason to delay since Cody had already turned two.

He'd allow Claire a few minutes of privacy with the boy, then he'd drive them all into town to get the marriage license before the courthouse closed for the day. Because she might be too proud to have folks find out the reason for her sudden marriage, Claire surely wouldn't want an elaborate wedding.

And a wait would cause a separation from the boy that he was also certain she wouldn't want. If they got the license today, they might be able to go ahead with the formalities in the next few days. He knew most of the judges in this part of Texas. If Claire would rather have a preacher do the ceremony, he'd look one up.

Satisfied with what he'd accomplished, Logan picked up the file and carried it back to lock in his desk. He paused to glance through the prenuptial agreement he'd had his lawyer draw up earlier in the week, but elected to leave it locked in the drawer with the file.

In it was the promise to allow Claire to adopt Cody. If she'd marry him without forcing him to sign this, he'd feel more comfortable. Not even he wanted to start a marriage with a prenup if word of honor was enough. And, there was always the chance that he'd misjudged Claire completely. If he had, then a break of her vows would entitle him to break his word to her.

He felt a nettle of guilt over that, but there were certain women who couldn't be trusted. Claire Ryan appeared completely trustworthy, but then, so had his mother. He'd trusted her too, though he'd been a naive little boy at the time. He'd been too trusting and naive a couple of times when he'd been in his early twenties, but he'd wised up. At thirty-two, he was years past that kind of foolishness.

Nowadays, he automatically conferred skepticism and mistrust on any woman he was interested in, unless she proved herself undeserving of it. Cody's mother, Farrah, hadn't had a scrap of honor, so he was rightly cautious of Claire, whatever he'd been able to find out about her.

Claire Ryan still had a few things to prove to him before he'd feel comfortable allowing her to adopt Cody. Whatever he'd said to her about her ability to live up to her commitments, he'd seen that mutinous flare in her pretty blue eyes. He'd known the moment he'd seen it that she was capable of filing for divorce once Cody became her legal son.

Which would defeat the purpose of marrying her to solve his problems with his nephew and to have a wife to get heirs. And, Claire wasn't quite the shy submissive flower he'd taken her for. The woman had managed to say a couple of things that had made his conscience squirm.

But then, he'd blindsided her with this, and she was upset. He'd allow her to blow off a little steam because her temper didn't trouble him. He'd braced himself for tears, so it was a distinct relief that she'd merely shown anger. At least he knew she had enough pride not to automatically resort to tears to get her way.

Logan finished with the paperwork he'd been doing when Claire and the boy had arrived, then went in search of his bride-to-be. He remembered she'd left her things beside the chair, so he went back to the den for them.

He found her in Cody's room, where she was sitting on the floor cross-legged with the boy in her lap as they looked through one of the oversized picture books he'd had the decorator supply.

Claire was dressed conservatively in a long-sleeved white blouse that was tucked into her belted and neatly creased khaki slacks. She'd worn simple sandals and had painted her toenails a tasteful pink. Her hair was a rich, dark brown, but her skin was city pale.

She had fine, even facial features, fairly straight teeth, but she wore almost no makeup. With a little effort and a more stylish haircut than the simple straight hair that fell to the top of her shoulder blades, she'd be striking. He noted again that she was petite and well-proportioned, but it was her long legs and her tantalizingly full breasts that he appreciated most.

He hadn't needed an investigator to tell him that she was nothing like her promiscuous stepsister. Though he was far from handsome, he knew the look women got when they had certain thoughts. Claire hadn't shown even an inkling of those. She was either not attracted to him at all or she didn't have enough experience to automatically consider him in terms of a potential affair.

And that was another reason he'd chosen her. The moment a woman found out he was rich *and* single, she zeroed in. Claire didn't seem at all interested in either him or his money, apart from how it affected the boy, and her chaste lifestyle was one he automatically respected.

He figured because of her reaction to him so far that she'd never fall wildly in love with him, which was fine. He wouldn't feel as if he'd cheated her when he didn't love her wildly back.

Claire looked up to see him in the doorway, and he noted the subtle way she stiffened. The boy must have felt it because he looked up to peer over the top of the oversized book. The moment he saw Logan, Cody turned in Claire's lap to bury his face shyly in her shirtfront. She calmly closed the book and set it on the bookshelf behind her.

Leery of startling the boy, Logan kept his voice low. "Is he in better humor?"

Claire offered a faint smile. "Much better. Perhaps if you'd come over and sit down, he wouldn't be so intimidated by your s-i-z-e."

The fact that she'd spelled out the word tickled him. He brought her things and put them beside her. But instead of sitting on the floor like a woman or a kid might, Logan hunkered down and gave Claire a prompting look. After all, she was the expert and she'd just been generous enough to give advice. Though she might be doing it solely to help the boy, Logan would benefit.

"An s-m-i-l-e might help, Mr. Pierce. They look like this," she added and widened her own stiff smile.

Logan felt the sting to his pride. Was she poking fun at him? He studied her face and it seemed a little too guileless to be believed. He wasn't sure how to take this. If she was teasing him, he automatically took a dim view of it, though he did manage what he was sure was a more pleasant expression.

''Hey there, Cody.'' His greeting to the boy felt awkward and that was a surprising frustration. He'd expected something more man-to-man, an instinctive understanding because the boy was blood kin and they were both male.

He'd have to remember that the child had had mostly female influence in his life, so it might take a little longer for them to hit it off.

Cody turned his head and sneaked a look at him before he shyly hid his face again. Claire eased the boy a little away from herself.

''Say hello to your uncle Logan, sweetheart,'' she coaxed. ''He's the one who got you the beautiful book.''

As if being bought a book was a big deal to the kid, the boy looked over at him, a little less mistrustfully. But there was no hello, so Logan took a chance.

''Have you tried out the rocking horse?''

Cody merely blinked at that, but Claire shook her head.

''Ever seen a real pony?'' he tried next, and felt a flush creep along his cheekbones. It felt odd and somehow unmanly to talk to the boy this way. And he was stumbling around at it in front of Claire, who handled the kid easily and with a familiarity that he suddenly doubted he'd ever have.

It was a reminder not only of her power over his nephew, but that however dense the judge had been, Claire Ryan was the one person qualified to continue raising this boy. Logan might have won the legal right, but morally, Claire was the one who'd earned it. The hard way.

Knowing that did nothing to ease his sense of guilt for pushing to get the boy, and it annoyed him that the guilt he'd tried to ignore about blackmailing Claire suddenly spiked. He had good motives, and he meant to cause only good to come out of this, but he'd charged into something private and special to lay claim to a child whom he was using to coerce a woman into marriage.

He'd taken away Claire's choices with both things, and once she married him, he'd be after even more things that she might not have chosen to give him otherwise. It was all he could do now to tamp down his conscience to a more bearable level.

"We'll go see a real pony when we get back from town," he said gruffly, then lifted his gaze to Claire, compelled to keep pushing despite his feelings of guilt. "Are you done thinkin' about this? It'd be best to get to town before the courthouse closes."

Claire had been privately enjoying the big man's effort to somehow connect with the boy, and she'd been unwillingly touched by it. It was clear Logan was trying, and it was also clear that he probably had no experience with two-year-olds. She'd seen the flush that had darkened his tanned skin and again felt as if she was glimpsing something—embarrassment this time—that humanized the man and made him less objectionable. Until he'd mentioned the courthouse.

''Surely you realize how bizarre that idea is, Mr. Pierce. Marriages are hard enough to make and keep when both people know each other and are in love. You and I are complete strangers. We aren't even attracted to each other. There's not a drop of chemistry.''

Those dark, dark eyes gentled a fraction. ''Speak for yourself, *Ms. Ryan.* As I see it, we've got as good a chance to have something worthwhile as the fools who imagine they're in love and can't keep their hands off each other. At least neither of us will whine about it and go to war when the fire goes out.''

Claire's brows went up. ''You're amazingly cynical.''

''I'm amazingly right. And the boy needs two parents. I've made my proposal.''

Claire felt even more trapped, only this time the trap felt brutally tight. ''So,'' she began a little hoarsely, "no marriage, no nothing after Monday morning."

His hard gaze fell briefly from hers. It was a telltale sign of guilt that gave her a sliver of hope until it came back up and drilled harshly into hers.

"That's about the size of it."

Claire felt a gurgle of hilarity come up and realized she'd been distraught for so long and felt so pressured now that she was on the verge of becoming a bit hysterical.

This brute was determined to get his way, and as insane as his so-called marriage "proposal" was, she felt too desperate to hold out for long. If she could bring herself to go through with it, the only thing that would make being married to Logan Pierce bearable and worth the sacrifice, was that she could adopt Cody. Then she'd be free to walk away with *her son* and Logan Piece would have no legal way to force either of them to do anything.

But before she allowed him to rush her off to the courthouse, she needed to hear a few assurances. After all, getting the license didn't mean they were married. She might be able to string him along a few days and delay the ceremony for quite a while if she gave in this time with at least a semblance of grace.

Claire lifted Cody to his feet and pointed him toward the toy box. "Why don't you see what toys are in the toy box while your uncle and I have a talk?" Just as the boy started in that direction, Claire remembered their manners and caught him.

"Ooops, Mommy forgot."

Cody looked at her expectantly, and she gave him an encouraging smile. "Can you tell Uncle Logan thank you for the book and the pretty room?"

Cody looked over at Logan. Just when Claire thought he couldn't overcome his shyness, he said a quiet, "Fanks." He struggled to suppress a bashful smile before he turned away and scampered over to the toy box to look inside.

Claire got smoothly to her feet before Logan could straighten to his full height, just in case he'd found enough manners in the last little while to offer her his hand. She didn't want to touch or be touched by him.

Now that Cody was completely absorbed by the wooden truck he'd pulled out of the toy box, she edged away from Logan to step out into the hall. She wanted to stay close enough to keep an eye on Cody, but she also didn't want the boy to overhear her talk with Logan. Surely they could keep their voices down.

Logan went along with her, though it was clear by his frown when she stopped outside the door, that he wasn't sure why either of them were just standing there.

"I need you to answer some things, but I realize we're short on time," she began briskly. "I'd appreciate the truth, Mr. Pierce."

He seemed to bristle. "You'll get it."

Claire lifted her brows but didn't challenge that. "Are you capable of marital fidelity?"

"I've sowed my wild oats," he said, and his voice was again a growl.

Her brows climbed higher. "I sincerely hope none of those wild oats show up. I'm already committed to raise one child that I didn't conceive."

His expression had just started to go stony when she posed the next question. "What assurance do I have that you'll allow me to adopt Cody?"

"We can do a prenup."

Claire nodded. "Are you capable of attending the church of my choice on Sundays, or are you a complete heathen?"

That one must have caught him off guard because it wiped the stoniness from his face. "I can and I'm not."

"You're not what, a heathen?"

"That's right. I'll go."

"I'll expect you to set a good example."

"Done."

"Will you heed my opinions and take them seriously, or are you expecting a door-mat?"

Now she got what had to be the closest thing to a smile that Logan Piece might be capable of. "I reckon my hopes are fading on that."

Claire almost laughed. His answer made her like him, and she hadn't expected that. It was the only nice surprise in this whole mess. Nevertheless, she pressed on toward something that was a little more delicate than everything else.

"We've talked about fidelity, but I hope you understand that intimacy is out of the question until we know each other and have a high level of trust. *Very* high."

"Fine with me, too," he said, and Claire felt like heaving a huge sigh of relief. Until she heard what he said next.

"But we'll share a bed from the wedding night on. I won't have it get around that I married a woman who wouldn't sleep with me.''

Claire couldn't disguise her horror. ''How would anyone find out? It's none of their business anyway.''

''I've got a housekeeper. Unless you want to fire a woman who'll retire next year, and take care of both the boy and this house by yourself, that's the way it'll have to be.''

Claire felt a quiver of sensual peril that made her mouth go dry. She couldn't share a bed with a stranger, especially not *this* stranger. If the problem was Elsa finding out, then she'd make certain Elsa never had reason to suspect. It should be a fairly simple problem to solve.

''Anything else you have to know right now?'' His voice was brusque. ''We've got a little over an hour, and it takes forty-five minutes to get downtown.''

Claire had been saving this last question, hoping for a reprieve. ''Won't I need a birth certificate?''

That gave him pause, but it didn't deter him as effectively as she'd hoped.

"We'll see when we get there. Better collect the boy," he said, then nodded toward Cody, who'd pulled out two more trucks and was now playing with them on the carpet. "If he needs to take something along, let him bring whatever he wants. I don't want a problem with him at the courthouse."

"He won't be a problem," she said, then rushed back into the room to get another fresh diaper out of the cloth bag Logan had brought in with him.

As she readied Cody for the drive, she prayed earnestly that they wouldn't be able to get a marriage license without her birth certificate. There had to be some way to slow all this down without risking even a brief separation from Cody.

Claire felt doomed. Apparently this county didn't require a birth certificate since she had a valid Texas driver's license to verify her age and identity as a U.S. citizen. Before she could even begin to get her racing heart under control, they were on their way back to the ranch.

Cody was in his car seat in the back of the SUV, contentedly making truck engine sounds as he ran a small pickup on the inside of the vehicle door. He'd actually allowed Logan to carry him out of the courthouse, and he'd seemed to enjoy the novelty of the much higher vantage point the big man's height afforded him.

Claire was torn between wanting the boy to stay close only to her and wanting him to feel comfortable and secure with the man the court had given custody of him to. She'd rarely felt jealous of anyone, so her jealous feelings now were another unhappy surprise.

If Logan had approached her differently and had made some effort at having a family relationship with the boy that hadn't put her in this awful position—if he hadn't used blackmail—she was certain she would have graciously shared the boy and been glad to do it. She would have allowed Logan to be a natural part of the boy's life and she would have done everything possible to facilitate that.

Instead, Logan Pierce had pushed and bullied to get what he'd wanted, and she hated that Cody's small acceptance of him would reward him yet again for being a tyrant.

It was difficult to accept that Logan was already getting everything, including her now, but she focused instead on the idea that Cody could benefit greatly from having a good relationship with his uncle. Because the court hadn't given her or the boy any other choice, she had to make the best of things for Cody's sake.

And unless there was some way to get Logan to back off his marriage demand, it would be best for Cody if she tried to get along with the man. Doing what she could to make things run smoothly between the three of them seemed to be her only sensible option.

Until she could legally become Cody's mother. Keeping that in mind would make it easier to tolerate all this. The very moment she had legal standing with the court, Logan Pierce wouldn't find it quite so easy to bully and manipulate her. He'd have to develop a few sterling character qualities if he meant to persuade her to stay married to him.

And judging by what she'd seen so far, the only way Logan Pierce would ever possess such sterling qualities would be if he could find a few of them to buy and tape to his body.

CHAPTER FOUR

THEY arrived back at the ranch in time to wash up for supper at 6:00 p.m. The wooden highchair in the formal dining room complemented the long, polished table that was now covered with a beautiful damask tablecloth. A lavish bouquet of artificial flowers provided the centerpiece, and the china and crystal were elegant. Claire felt as if she should have dressed up, but Logan didn't suggest it. In fact, he was still in his work clothes, and she appreciated the lack of formality.

Cody needed the height of the highchair, but not the tray. Claire moved his small place setting and placemat to the table between Logan's place at the head and the place set for her to his right. She unhooked the tray and set it on a nearby chair before she helped Cody climb up.

If either Logan or Elsa objected to this arrangement, neither of them commented on it. Logan slid the boy's chair up to the table, then took another moment to seat her. Claire covered her surprise by tucking a small fingertip towel she'd brought into the neck of Cody's shirt to serve as a bib.

Once they were settled, Elsa served the food and left the room. Logan reached for the meat plate. Claire delicately cleared her throat, then repeated it a little more insistently when the sound failed to get Logan's attention.

Logan stopped, holding the meat plate between them, and glanced at her. Claire stared meaningfully at him as she lifted her hands and laced her fingers together in a prayer pose. Beside her, Cody followed suit, pressing his little palms together and scrunching his eyes closed.

Logan stayed frozen a moment more as he took this in, then set the meat plate aside. His dark brows lowered in a frown. Claire closed her eyes and bowed her head slightly to repeat the simple, childlike prayer that Cody echoed. She paused at the end of the prayer and Cody called out an eager Amen.

When she opened her eyes and looked over at Logan, she saw he hadn't moved. From the look of him, he hadn't bowed his head or closed his eyes. But he was staring at Cody and she caught the unmistakable combination of chagrin and gentleness in his eyes. Almost as if the little boy's recitation had both chastened and moved him.

Claire couldn't help but like Logan for that. Perhaps the man wasn't so bad. Perhaps he had potential. But then she remembered what he'd said about *her* potential and was irritated all over again.

She took the meat plate he handed her and served herself before she passed it back and picked up her knife and fork to slice off a small piece of steak to put on the boy's plate. None of them spoke while she cut Cody's steak into bite-sized pieces. She took the other food dishes Logan passed her and served both herself and Cody before she handed them back.

Cody was normally a good eater, and none of that changed tonight. He wasn't particularly adept with his fork, but she did no more than remind him to use it from time to time. It amused her to watch Logan's face as Cody picked up a piece of steak and laboriously stuck it onto the tines of his fork before he lifted it to his mouth.

She wondered if Logan would say anything, but he didn't. Instead, he seemed enthralled by the whole process as Cody worked his way through his meal. Claire was unwillingly touched by that too. However much a tyrant he was, Logan wasn't fussing with Cody's little errors, and he didn't make any comments or complaints to her about them either.

It was a fact that anyone who wanted to impress her had only to treat Cody well. Had this manipulator figured that out, or was all this genuine?

Claire couldn't seem to talk herself out of the notion that what she was seeing and sensing in Logan was real. Though he'd started out remote and disapproving toward the boy, he'd been more than making up for it since. Cody was losing some of his bashfulness with the big man, and his attention wandered Logan's way frequently, though he stayed close to Claire for security.

After supper, Logan helped her bring their things in from her car before he drove it away to park in his huge garage. Claire hadn't been able to bring everything of Cody's, and she'd hoped to use that as an excuse to come back to Pierce Ranch if things hadn't gone well that day. She'd brought all of Cody's clothes and many of his books and toys had been included, but not the larger things.

She still wasn't certain how well today had gone. Yes, it looked as if there was a way to remain an important part of Cody's life, but it would come at a heavy cost. On the other hand, this child was more than worth the hazard of marrying an arrogant man she couldn't love and tolerating that marriage for as long as it took to become Cody's legal mother.

Perhaps she should consider Logan's proposal a blessing. It was just so hard to cave in and agree to marry the man one moment before she absolutely had to, though the impulse to spare herself for as long as possible made her feel selfish for considering her comfort rather than Cody's.

When she finished putting Cody's things away in his new room, she went into the guest room she'd been given across the hall. She unpacked the clothes she'd brought along for herself, just in case, and she was glad now that she had. She'd included a small variety of things, so there was enough to last four or five days if need be.

How long could she put off marrying Logan? Now that she felt at least a little less leery about the boy being around him, her worries about being around Logan herself were growing.

Again she wondered how on earth she'd be able to tolerate even holding his hand, much less allowing full intimacy. Though he'd left her no choice, it didn't seem quite honest to accept his marriage proposal when she wasn't even marginally attracted to him.

Perhaps she could find something about Logan that she considered personally attractive. She thought again about sharing a bed with him and felt that same quiver of sexual peril, only this time, it didn't feel half as objectionable as it had.

A little unsettled by that, Claire finished in the guest room, and went back to Cody's room. He'd managed to scatter toys all over the carpet around the toy box, so she helped him pick them up.

They found Logan in the den, but when Claire saw he was using the phone, she and Cody remained standing in the hall to give him privacy. The moment he saw them waiting, he finished the call.

Since Logan had mentioned showing Cody a pony, Claire had changed out of her sandals into her sneakers. She'd only visited a ranch a few times, but she knew enough about them to be certain she wouldn't want to wear sandals too far away from the house.

Logan crossed the room to them and Cody edged a little behind Claire. She couldn't blame the boy. Logan's size was still something she found difficult to adjust to. It wasn't only that he was tall, but he looked powerful and strong. He was lean, but every bit of him was solid with muscle. The kind of men she usually saw looked soft by comparison. And common.

Though she didn't consider Logan handsome, he had a male charisma that made him a standout. His macho look merely added to that. She felt so small and completely feminine by comparison that her stomach began to flutter with an odd attraction, and she felt a ripple of dismay.

"Think the boy's ready to see the pony?"

Claire tried to smile, but it felt stiff. "I'm sure he'll love that."

Logan looked down at Cody. "How 'bout we go see your pony, son?"

Cody had been holding Claire's hand with both of his, and Logan's sudden focus on him made him bashfully hide his face behind her hand.

Claire felt a spark of sympathy. The man couldn't help that he was big and had a harsh, intimidating look. And he was clearly trying to be kind to the boy. Cody's reaction suddenly made her feel embarrassed enough for Logan to try to help.

"Your uncle Logan would like to take you to see a pony. That's a very sweet thing for him to do, Cody. Wouldn't you like to go?"

The boy gave a small nod, but still used her hand as a shield. She gave Logan an apologetic look. "He's not trying to be rude.

He'll be entirely different once he knows you better.''

It surprised her that Logan didn't seem convinced. In fact, he looked at her in a way that hinted at mistrust, and she felt offended by that. Did he think she was influencing the child not to like him?

''I reckon we might as well go on out,'' he said, then started down the hall to lead the way through the house.

They ended up in a kitchen large enough to land a small plane in, and every surface was immaculate. Logan crossed to the wall pegs beside the back door and took down a black Stetson before he glanced back at them and reached to open the door.

He waited for them to walk out ahead of him, then he followed and closed the door. Once they were on the back patio, he walked on the other side of Cody.

''Sneakers are fine for the city or the house, but you and the boy'll need boots.

Hats, too, and some sturdy clothes. Don't bother with tourist stuff.''

Claire glanced his way briefly but he added nothing more enlightening so she let her gaze stray back toward their destination. The headquarters seemed gigantic, and she had no idea which building or barn was which. The network of corrals was laid out in neat precision.

Though there were many large shade trees crowded nearer the house, they gradually thinned out as they walked on. The creek to the east in the distance was marked by a line of trees, but the whole place was like an oasis compared to the miles of empty rangeland around it.

The air still carried much of the heat of the day, but it seemed cooler out here than in the cement-surround of the city, perhaps by a good ten degrees. Dust still hung in the air that also carried the sounds and smells of cattle and horses.

All of which seemed huge and potentially dangerous to Claire as she and Cody walked with Logan past a few on their way down one of the alleys that bisected the pens. Claire was so accustomed to seeing cattle and horses from the safe distance of the highway that this close up look was unnerving.

In the corral to their right were horses who looked so big that their shod hooves appeared to be the size of dinner plates. The cows in some of the pens on the left looked huge and heavy and intimidating.

Claire was suddenly worried, not for herself, but for the very small boy who was taking it all in with eyes that were round with awe. And since Cody was so very small, the animals must have seemed even more monster-sized to him. Claire made certain she had a firm grip on his hand. Beside them, Logan walked confidently, though he'd had to shorten his long stride considerably to accommodate the child.

For the first time Claire realized Logan wasn't such a giant out here. This was the world he worked in every day, and his larger than life stature fit perfectly. Now his ruggedness made him seem equal to the challenge of large animals and potentially dangerous situations. There was still plenty about him that overwhelmed her, but suddenly she was glad he seemed so rough and tough.

There was something reassuring about Logan, something that suggested a level of protection and competence that could ward off danger and overcome difficulty. He'd lived here all his life, and no doubt he could handle anything that came along. He'd certainly be able to assert a greater level of control over it all than she'd ever be able to.

The tender-skinned little hand in hers made Claire realize why she was pondering all this. Cody would grow up here, and she was absolutely certain that Logan would require the boy's almost constant involvement with everything to do with the ranch and ranch work.

But from what age? Two? She'd heard stories for years about children only a little older than Cody actually riding full-grown horses.

For Claire, an optimum age for Cody to be out in all this and at risk with large animals would be…ten. Ideally, twenty-one seemed the most agreeable.

Something told her that Logan meant to start the boy far sooner than age ten. Suddenly she knew that this little walk was the actual beginning of Cody's quick immersion into ranch life. The pony was merely the excuse to start right into the first stage.

And because Logan seemed to have almost no experience with small children, he probably didn't understand that Cody needed extra protection from the hazards of the very life he meant for the boy to live.

Claire didn't want this child anywhere near these monstrous animals without her constant supervision. And if Logan Pierce thought he was going to immerse this precious little boy in anything more risky than his nightly tub bath, he'd have to change his plan. She'd see to that.

They stopped at one of the corrals, which Claire at first thought was empty. Logan unlatched the gate and waited for her and Cody to go in ahead of him. Once inside, Claire saw the pony on the other side of a large water tank. She'd expected something only a little bigger than a large dog, but the pony was larger than she'd expected.

It had a dappled gray hide and a flowing white mane and tail. She had a scant moment to enjoy the sight of the pretty animal before it suddenly started in their direction at a trot.

Then the trot switched to a gallop and the pony gave a high bucking kick, which gave the impression of a rodeo bronc. If that wasn't bad enough, the little powerhouse charged straight at them.

Because Logan didn't immediately react to that, she suddenly realized she'd taken his protectiveness for granted. What good was Logan's rough and tough size if he didn't realize the danger? Because she did, Claire instantly snatched up Cody and pivoted to flee.

And crashed into Logan. Even more startled, Claire tried to move to the side and crowd behind his big body for refuge, but Logan's strong arms came tightly around both her and the boy to hold them immovable.

Alarmed, Claire glanced over her shoulder in time to see the pony skid to a halt just behind her.

Cody's excited shriek, "Pony!" further rattled her, but she realized a second later that it wasn't a shriek of fear but one of boyish delight.

Logan's voice was gravelly and low, but there was no mistaking his displeasure. "What the hell's this about?"

Claire looked up into his harsh face and saw the snap of anger in his dark eyes. He released her to neatly pull the wiggling boy from her arms. Claire reached belatedly for Cody, but there was no way to reclaim him without getting into a tug of war.

Logan stepped past her with the boy and set him on the ground in front of the pony before he hunkered down to supervise the introduction. Cody was all but dancing in place with excitement. The pony tossed its head, and Claire reflexively reached toward the boy.

Logan must have caught her sudden move in his side vision because he turned his head to look up at her.

"If you can't keep outta this, get out of the pen," he growled, and Claire felt his rebuke like a slap. Anger and acute shame scorched her face and she forced herself to stay quiet, her fists clenched in readiness to protect Cody if the pony gave any hint of a dangerous move.

Claire thought she'd outgrown her fear of horses, but it was obvious now that she hadn't. Her strong feelings of protectiveness toward Cody had only heightened the old fear, and Claire was belatedly aware that her overreaction had been completely uncalled for.

The pony was actually very gentle with the little boy, as if he understood there was a difference between a small child and an adult. Claire tried to relax and remind herself that Logan was certainly big enough and experienced enough to protect Cody, but she couldn't seem to help that she was still shaking.

Logan coached the boy to stroke the inquisitive pony's nose and Claire cringed, vowing to intervene if the pony tried to bite. Instead, the pony eased a little closer as if it enjoyed the attention. It appeared remarkably calm and mild-mannered now.

A few moments of that and Logan slowly rose to his full height, lifting the boy as he did. Before Claire realized what he was about to do, Logan promptly set Cody on the pony's sleek back.

Claire bit her lip painfully, so anxious about this that it was all she could do to keep silent. The pony had no halter, no bridle, and there was no rope. So when Logan took his hands away from Cody and let the boy balance on the pony's back, anchored there only by his little fingers gripping the pony's mane, she couldn't prevent her protest.

"Don't—please don't let him fall."

Logan gave every appearance of ignoring her. Cody was grinning hugely, and before Claire realized what would happen next, Logan placed his hand under the pony's jaw and walked away with him.

Leading and controlling the pony with nothing more than a loose grip!

Claire started to follow then made herself stop, suddenly worried about startling the animal. She watched like a hawk as Logan calmly led the pony across the corral, keeping careful track of the boy before turning at the fence to lead the pony along the rails. Claire tried to calm herself as she listened to Logan coach the boy to sit up straighter and squeeze the pony's sides with his legs.

Cody not only managed to stay on, he was crowing with pleasure and excitement. He did try to squeeze the pony's sides with his legs, but then he'd get excited and drum his heels against the pony until Logan again corrected him.

Logan didn't stop until he'd led the pony around the corral three times. Claire was certain she'd barely breathed during that time. She literally couldn't calm down, not even when Logan reached the gate and lifted Cody off the pony to stand him on the ground.

She finally made her legs move, dismayed that they were shaky and weak. She was still frightened but now she was so deeply ashamed of herself that this was easily the biggest humiliation of her adult life.

Until they'd come to the corral, Logan had seemed awkward with Cody, but there'd been no awkwardness just now. Logan had handled it all masterfully. He certainly knew what he was doing, and it was easy to conclude that Cody had been perfectly safe the

entire time. The pony was obviously well-
trained and Logan had been in complete control of both the animal and the little boy.

Cody's high-pitched, "No! I wanna ride!
More ride!" was a signal that Cody had lost
his bashfulness with his uncle.

Truth to tell, Logan had neatly won Cody
over the moment he'd put the boy on the
pony, and Claire felt a nick of hurt. And
Cody's surprising, very vocal tantrum now
prompted her to realize that nothing she'd
ever done or provided for Cody had elicited
as much enthusiasm as the pony—or this
much defiance when it was taken away.

Cody's little face was a mutinous red and
his cheeks were streaked with fat tears.

"No, no, no! I wanna ride!" he went on
as Logan calmly turned the pony away.

Logan chuckled and lifted Cody off the
ground to swing him up onto his arm.

"That's enough ridin' for one night, son,"
he said, untroubled that Cody was howling

and that his sneakered toes pummeled Logan's hip in protest.

The big man walked leisurely to the gate and unlatched it as calmly as if Cody were quietly riding on his arm instead of throwing a world-class tantrum. Claire hurried along after them and managed to squeeze through the opening just before Logan absently closed the gate.

Everything in Logan's body language announced that he was completely ignoring her, and the way he'd just closed the gate without even pausing for her to walk through suggested that he'd forgotten she was tagging along, though she knew he hadn't forgotten her for a moment.

Sick with humiliation and regret over her earlier overreaction, Claire pretended not to notice the slight. Perhaps there was a way to somehow smooth things over, some way to appear less cowardly.

Logan was unhappy with her, and she realized even more fully the consequences of what had happened at the corral. He was a rancher who probably loved his outdoor lifestyle. There wasn't a doubt in her mind that he would insist on raising Cody to be the same.

But having a chickenhearted wife would complicate his plans for the boy. His order to leave the corral if she couldn't ''keep out of this'' explained the reason he completely ignored her now, and also let her know that he was not only disgusted with her but possibly furious.

Though she'd already decided to do everything she could to prevent Logan from exposing Cody to the dangers presented by large animals, her upset over the pony was proof—even to her—that she was leery even in less hazardous situations.

Claire couldn't quite appreciate the irony of hoping to find a way to delay their marriage when there was every chance now that Logan would take back his proposal.

Halfway to the house, Cody's protests wound down. As if things weren't already upsetting enough and completely out of her control, the little boy laid his head sweetly on Logan's shoulder.

Claire sensed that Cody had accepted the big man and she felt her heart clench with pain and raw jealousy. How easily Logan had accomplished it, despite his inexperience with children. As powerless and desperate as she'd felt before over losing to Logan in court and then being blackmailed into marriage, nothing compared with the powerlessness and desperation—and the sense of loss—she felt now.

Another glimpse of Logan's harsh profile set off a new wave of anxiety, and Claire walked on resolutely at his side, heartsick.

The sight of Cody's dark head resting so trustingly on Logan's shoulder confirmed the worst thing of all—that Logan Pierce had just stolen the heart of the person she loved most in the world.

CHAPTER FIVE

CLAIRE positively loathed people who punished with silence. There was nothing more unsettling than being balanced on the razor edge of the worries and the insecurities that silences dealt to their victims. As far as she was concerned, silence was a cruel and dishonest way to handle a disagreement.

But what aggravated her more than anything was that she wasn't certain how wise she would be to challenge Logan on it. If anyone else had given her the silent treatment, she wouldn't have tolerated it. But since Cody had so quickly gotten over his bashfulness with the big man, Logan might not need her any more to help facilitate his relationship with the boy.

The fact that she'd managed to land on Logan's bad side so soon made her worry that he'd cancel his marriage proposal, or would the next time she made a wrong move.

Hence her chastened silence as she gave Cody his bath then read to him before his uncle came in to tell him goodnight and solemnly supervised as Claire tucked the boy in the baby bed.

She'd already realized that she'd have to walk on eggshells for however long it took to actually marry the man and complete all the legal steps to adopt Cody. It just hadn't occurred to her that Logan would be quite this unreasonable, though she should have expected this. Tyrants practiced a number of excesses when faced with less than absolute compliance with their dictates.

He had yet to say one word to her directly, but in the interest of good will, she'd politely informed him earlier about the details of Cody's nightly routine. First that it was time for the boy's bath, and that she'd read to him a bit afterward before his general bedtime of eight-thirty, so Logan would know when to come to Cody's room to tell him good night.

Now that she'd finished with everything and they'd both got through the goodnight ritual with Cody, they stepped into the quiet hall. The moment of reckoning was swiftly approaching. However careful Claire was about riling Logan again, there was no way she'd tolerate letting the night go by without a definite resolution.

Logan moved past her and strode down the hall to the main part of the house. Claire lingered near the partially opened door to Cody's room to make certain he'd truly settled down and would go right to sleep. Though at home she'd already moved him into a regular bed, she'd chosen to put him in the baby bed at least for tonight.

Since this was a strange house, the baby bed might give them both a better sense of security. Unless Cody decided to climb out. That's why she lingered quietly in the hall just out of sight. Fortunately, the excitement of the day and the fact that Cody hadn't gotten his usual full nap ensured that within ten minutes he was fast asleep.

Claire took a steadying breath and went in search of Logan. Elsa apparently went home every night just after she finished clearing things away from supper, so there was little chance of anyone overhearing.

The reminder sent a fine shiver of tension through her as she realized that she and Logan would be the only ones in the house except for the sleeping boy. Something about that sent the shiver of tension deeper.

She found Logan in his den. His expression was still the same flinty closed one he'd worn since their visit to the corrals. Claire resented that, but she'd have to keep a tight rein on her irritation and be so, *so* careful with this. His marriage proposal was only a few hours old. And easily—far too easily— revoked. If he hadn't changed his mind already.

Claire stood hovering in the doorway for several annoying seconds, then reached over to rap her knuckles on the open door. It seemed to take a significant number of moments more for Logan to look up.

His black gaze sliced swiftly over her, and she realized it was probably the only greeting she would receive from the cretin. The man was arrogance personified.

''I think we need to discuss a few things,'' she told him, careful to keep her voice calm as she walked on into the room and crossed to his desk.

He watched her every step of the way, but this time his gaze alighted here and there and she felt a startling warmth in each place that sent a fresh shiver of tension through her. The fact that her tension was at least mildly sexual did nothing to calm her jangling nerves.

Logan leaned back in his chair as if he were waiting for her to speak. She noted there was no invitation to sit down, and she hated his rudeness. He still hadn't responded to her statement, which sent her temper up another notch.

"I don't care for this silent treatment," she announced, though she was careful to keep her tone conversational. "If you're upset with me, say so and say why."

Logan didn't respond or react for another few seconds. Just when she thought she couldn't keep her irritation to herself another moment, he spoke.

"I won't tolerate another stunt from you like that one at the corral."

Claire wasn't certain she'd heard right. "Stunt?"

Logan rested his elbows on the chair arms but the glitter in his gaze told her he was anything but relaxed.

"If you mean to keep the boy from taking to the life out here, you'll be gone."

Claire was thunderstruck. What she'd had a hint of earlier—that Logan mistrusted her—was so clear to her now that it might as well have been spelled out on a neon sign. "What are you talking about?"

"I won't let you scare him off," he said in a low, gravelly drawl, but what he said next was a blatant threat. "Don't ever act up like that again."

Claire gave her head a dazed shake. It shocked her that he hadn't realized she'd genuinely been afraid when the pony had rushed at them. Because he hadn't realized the extent of her fear for the boy, much less her fear for herself, she didn't want to confess both things to him. No sense offering that kind of personal information to an adversary unless there was no way to avoid it.

After all, he might consider her fears for the boy reasonable, but *her* fear of the pony would seem ridiculous to him. He'd probably never been afraid of anything in his life.

"I was...protecting Cody," she said quietly. "The pony seemed...wild. At first."

"Do you think I'd put the boy in danger?" The angry glitter in Logan's eyes was more pronounced as he slowly rose to his feet.

Oh my, that idea had mightily offended him. Unrushed, he started around the big desk and she stifled the urge to move back.

Claire didn't dare answer his question with a straightforward ''yes,'' so she tried to think of a reply that was just as true, but more tactful. And she couldn't lie because she sensed he'd see right through it.

As he stopped little more than arm's length away, she realized he was so angry that anything she said could be disastrous, whether she told him the truth or lied her head off. She made a careful start.

''I doubt you'd put him in danger on purpose, but you don't seem to have much experience with small children. I don't know you well enough to be certain you fully realize how small and immature Cody is, and how risky it will be for a child his age to be exposed to much of the rougher side of ranch life. Animals are unpredictable, are they not?''

Logan lifted his big fists to rest them on his lean hips. Claire tried not to let that subtly intimidating pose rattle her. His voice was still low and gravelly.

''So it follows that if you can make him afraid, you think I'll just hand him over to you to take back to city life.''

Her attempt at tact was a rousing failure. On the other hand, she was more than a little guilty of wanting to be able to just take Cody home and keep him all to herself—and to somehow escape Logan's marriage mandate—so she couldn't truthfully deny everything he was accusing her of.

''What happened at the corral wasn't deliberate, Mr. Pierce.'' She could tell the moment the words were out of her mouth that they weren't enough to settle this.

''I won't deny that I'd rather have won in court,'' she admitted, ''or that I'd rather have Cody to myself. I won't deny that I

overreacted with the pony, but I wasn't trying to come between you and the boy, or to
make him afraid. That would be cruel, and I
think if you consider it a moment, you'll realize I wouldn't do that. After all, you're the
one Cody's legally obliged to stay with,
however he feels about it. I wouldn't sen-
tence him to sixteen years of fear and difficulty with you.''

It was hard to weather that brutal gaze as
it glittered and flared, hard to not look away
as Logan searched her face as if examining
it for any hint of dishonesty. She caught the
tiniest glimpse of perception.

''*You* were scared.''

The blunt words carried a hint of both curiosity and scorn. It was because of the scorn
that she tried to evade a complete answer.

''Perhaps 'overprotective' is a better
word.''

Now Logan tilted his head back as if to
study her in a slightly different way. ''That,

too. But you were scared. And not just for the boy, but for yourself.''

The closer he stood to her, the more impossible it became to somehow ward off the pressure to confess. Claire hoped he'd stop easing closer. Or that he might move away. Perhaps she should.

But then, Logan wasn't really moving closer, it just felt as if he were. Her tension was rapidly evolving into something else, and it was a distraction. But his body was like a big magnet, and her insides seemed to be reacting to the pull. It felt like a yearning, almost a craving.

She'd been upset for months, and these past few days had been awful. Today had been unbelievable, so she had to be mistaking all this. Since she hadn't been attracted to Logan at all, it didn't make sense that she'd suddenly be attracted to him now.

And she was too proud to just baldly confess her fear. Instead, she got out a stumbling, "I admit I haven't had much experience with horses."

Logan's stony expression eased and she sensed the harshness in him relent. His stern mouth actually curved a little, and the hard glitter in his eyes softened dramatically. It was an amazing transformation that made him suddenly...handsome.

"Well, now. Thanks, Claire, for the lesson."

His gravelly voice had gone smoother and lower, and it somehow moved through her leaving a trail of sparks. She felt too hypnotized by the sensation and the way he was looking at her to be sure how to take any of this, much less fathom what he was talking about.

"What lesson?"

"What you're like when you tell the truth. And what you're like when you lie to me. It's good that you're a bad liar."

Before she could respond to that, he added, "You probably got thrown from a horse and no one made you get over it."

Claire felt a modest wave of relief. He'd gotten it exactly right, and he showed no sign of scorn now. Something about the matter-of-fact way he'd said it made her feel freer to confirm his guess.

"I'm sure it's not an unheard of thing."

Logan actually smiled a little, and in spite of Claire's resistance to him, she thought it might be the sexiest smile she'd ever seen. But then he spoiled it.

"Well, honey, it's unheard of in these parts. You'll have to get over it quick."

What she'd thought was a major improvement in his hard-hearted, cold-blooded temperament and an understanding about her fear, was not. Riled, she forced a tight smile. "Oh my, I'm impressed. You make a decree, and suddenly it's done."

"Yes, ma'am. Right after breakfast tomorrow, it will be."

Was he toying with her? Or was he seriously trying to provoke her? After his punishing silence tonight, she wouldn't tolerate this.

"I'm not interested in horseback riding," she informed him stiffly. "After the list of wifely tasks you mandated this afternoon, I doubt I'll have much time for equestrian pursuits."

"You will if you're my wife."

Claire searched his face for any sign of a threat, but he looked more relaxed—and handsome—than she'd ever seen him, so she wasn't able to tell how serious he really was about this. Since he appeared to be having a little fun at her expense, perhaps she could return the favor.

"Is that right? Well, you left that little requirement off your order for a wife. Since you filled in all the available blanks when you placed your order, I'm afraid this little extra can't be guaranteed. And tomorrow might be a little soon anyway, even with overnight delivery."

SUSAN FOX

"You've got a smart mouth, Claire." Logan's voice was low and smooth, but there was no hint of displeasure in what he'd just said. If it was a criticism, it certainly didn't sound like one.

"We all have our good points," she said and primly laced her fingers together in front of her.

The small movement seemed to set him off and he reached for her clasped hands and took a half step closer. Claire reflexively pulled back, but his grip tightened gently. She looked down at their hands, then away.

The silence in the room was charged, as if someone had thrown a high voltage switch. His big hands were hot and hard with calluses, and heat radiated over her skin to pool in places where heat had never pooled before. A delicious weakness seemed to flow along with the heat, and Claire felt the first diabolical tendrils of desire.

"I don't expect impossible things from you, Claire," he said softly, but there was no way to miss the implacable edge in his voice when he added, ''but the things I want, I aim to have.''

Normally, words like those would have provoked her. Not that she wasn't provoked by them now, but she just didn't quite feel the fiery outrage she should have. The only thing that saved her from letting Logan know that his touch had undermined a little of her will, was the fact that a man like him was ruthless enough to shamelessly exploit it if she revealed it to him now.

She looked up to boldly meet his black gaze. ''I'm not surprised that you have aims and goals. So do others.'' Claire lifted a disapproving brow. ''Speaking as one of those others, I've been wondering. Aside from getting to raise Cody, what will I get out of this marriage? Besides a list of orders and decrees, that is?''

''I'm not an ungrateful man.''

She tried to pull her fingers from his as she took a step back.

"Ah. That certainly covers my concerns in reassuring detail," she said with soft sarcasm, aggravated because she realized it was her fingers that were holding on to his. She promptly released them.

Logan was still looking down at her, still sexy in spite of himself. "You'll have plenty of money, a fine home, kids of your own…"

"I'm not wild about raising kids of my own with a bossy, overbearing tyr—"

Logan had caught her fingers again and before she could get the word "tyrant" out, they were standing toe to toe and his big hands had dropped to grip her waist.

"You talk a lot, honey," he said as his dark head descended.

Claire was too shocked to turn her head in time to escape before his hard lips seized hers. There was nothing less than absolute male confidence in that kiss, and Claire was completely unprepared for how swiftly it happened. Or how swiftly she felt her body respond.

This was no polite introduction, it was a brand. First kisses weren't even remotely like this, and Claire was suddenly drowning in the wildness of it. The kiss deepened and went aggressively carnal. Never in her life had a man kissed her like this, but she'd known from the moment his mouth had taken possession of hers that there probably wasn't another man on the face of the earth who would have dared to.

Even worse, he'd managed to trigger a feminine instinct and sexual drive she hadn't suspected she possessed. Only dimly was the rational part of her aware of how shamelessly her body betrayed her.

She was so completely taken over that when Logan ended the kiss, it took her a dazed moment or two to realize that the whimper of loss she heard was her own. Logan's gruff voice was like a toll of doom.

"It's all over but the ceremony, Claire. We'll fly to Vegas tomorrow. Or Reno."

Claire blamed herself. What else would a barbarian like him think after a kiss like that? What did *she* think after a kiss like that? Was her brain even functioning yet? She grappled for a shred of sense.

''I h-haven't agreed to marry you,'' she whispered hoarsely, her brain still so short-circuited that she couldn't actually remember whether she'd officially agreed to marry him or not. Why was she so muddled?

Logan's chuckle was another warm stroke through her insides. ''Your body just said 'I do,' darlin'...and it's downright multilingual.''

Claire felt her face go a fiery red. Belatedly, she realized she was clinging to him, and that she was plastered so tightly against him that it was as if she'd melted and stuck to his clothes. Humiliation made her summon at least the illusion of recovered pride, and somehow she found the will to push away from him.

"At least one of us isn't heartless and cold-blooded," she said, annoyed that her voice sounded as breathless as she felt. She looked up into his dark eyes and hated him for looking so damnably handsome. "And tomorrow's too soon."

She could tell by the glitter in his dark eyes that he hadn't liked the "heartless and cold-blooded" dig.

"No reason to wait."

Now the grimness was coming over him again and she refused to be bullied by it. "I want it in writing about the adoption. And I'll want my own lawyer, a new one. That will take time."

It relieved her when he turned away and walked around his desk, taking that awful magnetism with him. She could finally get a full breath.

Claire watched as he unlocked a desk drawer, and she thought that odd until he pulled out a thin legal document and passed it across the desk.

It was a prenuptial agreement, and she wasn't truly surprised. This dictator would, of course, be prepared to block every escape. But as she scanned the pages, Claire felt as if she held in her hands the only sure guarantee that Cody would legally be hers.

Her anger cooled, and the resentment she felt toward Logan began to ebb away. She glanced up at him and saw he'd gone harsh again. The handsome man he'd been had vanished.

"This doesn't say how soon adoption could begin," she pointed out.

"It doesn't need to."

Logan had gone even more somber and Claire realized that he didn't truly want to be bound to a prenup at all, much less one that pinned him down to a timetable.

"I think it does. I'll need to find a lawyer to represent my interests, and there might be a few other things I'd like to have in it."

His stony expression didn't change. "The only thing that needs to be in the prenup is the thing I told you I'd give you: the right to adopt Cody. I won't agree to anything else.''

Claire was chilled by that. She could tell he was immovable on the subject, and they both knew she couldn't walk away from Cody. So that gave him all the power. Didn't he realize that his control over her would end the moment she adopted Cody?

Or did he have something else up his sleeve to deal with that problem later?

Claire couldn't imagine what he could use to get his way then, but whatever his secret weapon was, it certainly wouldn't involve a plan to suddenly turn into Mr. Wonderful.

She gave a grave nod and made her voice suitably quiet.

''You win, Mr. Pierce. I hope what you think you've won gives you satisfaction.''

A hardness came over him then, and his voice was low and rough and just as quiet as hers had been. ''It will, Miss Ryan. You'll guarantee it.''

Claire's temper fairly shouted a defiant *We'll see about that!* as she searched his flinty expression for a way around the iron will behind it. But then she had another thought that gave her pause.

All this had more to do with Logan than it did with Cody or her. Though Logan Pierce wasn't a handsome man, he was appealing enough, and he was a very rich man. He shouldn't have been so desperate for a wife that he'd have to blackmail a potential candidate. And yet he must be. Why else would a man like him do this?

Perhaps it was because she loved Cody so much and had taken such pains to see to the careful development of his character that she was suddenly reminded that not every child had been raised with that kind of care and loving attention.

Though the last thing she wanted to do was to feel compassion or pity for Logan Piece, she couldn't help but wonder what had made him the cold-blooded autocrat he was now.

It was probably nothing she'd ever know the reason for, and it wouldn't be prudent to indulge in that kind of speculation. Logan was old enough to realize he was a jerk and to have done something to improve himself. The fact that he hadn't was all she needed to know. In the long run, she didn't expect to be married to him long enough for it to matter.

Her soft, ''Good night,'' was at least polite, and she turned to walk from the room, glad beyond words that the wild kiss between them now seemed as if it had happened hours ago.

When she got to her room, she quickly readied herself for bed. Because she had a craving to be close to Cody, she found a soft blanket in the closet, then took it to slip into the boy's room and quietly closed the door. She'd sleep on top of the coverlet on the single bed. If Cody had a restless night, she'd be near enough to know it.

And, truth to tell, she was still so shell-shocked from the events of that day that she wanted the comfort of sleeping close to the boy.

Troubled, Claire laid in the small bed a long time thinking as she stared at the baby animals on the wallpaper by the glow of the nightlight.

And, despite her every effort to block it out, she remembered that kiss.

CHAPTER SIX

THAT soul-rocking, toe-curling, pride-pummeling kiss!

Heavens, it wasn't as if she'd never been kissed before. She had, and a couple of times the young man had been quite expert at it. Her problem now was that Logan's kiss last night had been peerless.

As Claire slipped into the guest room to dress just before six that next morning and thought about the day ahead, it wasn't difficult to remember that she objected to almost everything else about the man. Although he'd shown a bit of gentle potential where Cody was concerned, he was pretty much a zero in other areas.

Claire left her room to tiptoe back across the hall to check on Cody. He was usually up by 6:00 a.m., but he was still asleep and

130

didn't look as if he meant to wake up in the next few minutes. Claire was just about to retreat back into the hall to go back to her room, when she heard another door open.

It could only be Logan coming out of his bedroom. She didn't have long to wait before those heavy bootsteps thudded down the hall then on into Cody's room. The boy must have heard them in his sleep because he jerked awake.

"Mommy?" Cody was suddenly sitting up, looking curiously at the bars of the baby bed before he grabbed them and got to his feet. "Mommy!"

"Mommy's here," she said and walked to the bedside to lower the rails.

"I don't wanna bed for babies," Cody said as he fastened his arms around her neck and gave her a kiss.

Claire hugged him a moment, then eased him away. "We'll talk about that later. Why don't we get you changed and dressed? Say hello to your uncle Logan while I get your things.''

One look at Logan made Cody grab her and cuddle close to hide his face.

Well, good. Logan was back to square one with Cody, and Claire felt resentful enough toward him to be glad. It wouldn't hurt his Hellacious Highness to suffer a small setback or two. At least there was someone he'd have to work to win over.

Claire exempted herself from that. Logan had already ''won'' her over via blackmail, so he'd never bother to make any honest effort for her now. No doubt he had a history of blackmailing people he didn't pay a salary to. And anyway, how would he go about winning her over? He'd already declared that he wasn't interested in love, and without love, any attempt to win her over would amount to nothing more than manipulation, and she'd already had enough of that.

Claire again eased away from Cody, successfully this time, to reach for the clothes and fresh diaper she'd set out for him the night before. Once he was dressed and she'd taken him into the bathroom to wash his face and hands for breakfast, they rejoined Logan to go to the dining room.

Elsa had no sooner brought in their food and gone out than Logan spoke.

''Elsa'll keep an eye on the boy until the sitter gets here. We'll drive to San Antonio to pick up any clothes you need, then catch a flight for Vegas. We can be back by late afternoon.''

The man was truly bullheaded on the subject of a quickie marriage, but it was too early in the morning for decrees.

He'd already picked up a serving dish to hand to her, and it gave her some small satisfaction to lace her fingers together and bow her head. Beside her, Cody followed suit.

Eyes closed, she suppressed a smile when she heard the dish thud lightly to the table, and she began to calmly recite the little prayer. Oblivious to the dark currents that swirled silently between the two adults, Cody echoed the words and again finished with a cheery and eager ''Amen!'' at the end.

Claire opened her eyes and lifted her head. The solemn surprise on Logan's harsh face was a priceless depiction of a man who'd been blindsided by a toddler's prayer. And it was also a picture of a man who was fully aware that his decree had just been challenged by her refusal to acknowledge it. Now his dark brows lowered and he again reached for the plate to pass it to her. His voice was gruff.

''If you didn't bring something nice enough for the ceremony, you can get something when we get there.''

Claire served Cody some of the eggs and then herself. ''Did we or did we not, race to town yesterday to get a marriage license?''

''No reason to wait.''

The words were intended to be a veiled reminder of his ''multilingual'' crack the night before. She didn't have much to retaliate with.

"The license won't be legal for seventy-two hours," she said, then passed the serving dish back to him. He took it and virtually dumped the rest of the eggs onto his plate.

"There's no wait in Vegas. Which is why we'll get it over with today."

"I won't leave Cody with people he doesn't know. Not for a whole day."

Logan braced a forearm on the table and gave her a stern look. "That decision won't be yours to make until after the ceremony."

Stung, Claire turned her attention to serving herself and Cody. Logan's remark hung heavily in the air and the tension between them soared.

How could she even think about marrying a despot like him? She'd never be the kind of woman who'd allow a man to walk all over her, and it was only a matter of time— perhaps mere seconds—before her temper went cosmic.

Claire couldn't resist sneaking a peek at Logan, and she caught him staring at her. She also caught a shadow of guilt in his eyes before they shifted to Cody.

The fiery burn of anger and resentment cooled significantly as she sensed his regret. Whatever was going on in his chauvinist brain, that hint of guilt and regret was at least a chink in the wall.

If she was reading him right, then perhaps he wasn't quite the bully his dictates made him appear to be. Was there any way to persuade him to be at least a little more reasonable?

Claire knew exactly how Cody would react to the prospect of being left in a stranger's care for the day, and everything maternal in her was ready to go to war.

But that hint of humanness she'd just glimpsed in Logan kept her from becoming too militant. Yet. Her appetite was gone, and she did little more than push her food around on her plate. There was no conversation, which was fine by her, but it was a relief when Cody pulled off his bib and made a move to signal that he wanted out of his high chair.

Claire immediately eased her chair back and stood to help him. Seeing no reason for either her or Cody to loiter in the dining room while Logan finished his meal, she led the boy out of the dining room to the hall then on to his room.

She supervised Cody washing his hands, then dithered over what to do as he scampered back out into his room. Watching his excitement as he went directly to the big rocking horse, she wondered how she might spare him the upset of a strange babysitter. And just the thought of leaving him here for most of the day in a strange house with people he didn't yet know, was excruciating.

Claire didn't have any real hope of escaping Logan's plan to marry her in Vegas today, but perhaps she could still reason with him about Cody. She could call her friend,

Ann, in San Antonio. Ann's little boy was a frequent playmate of Cody's, so she might be willing to watch him for the day.

Meanwhile, there had to be a way to put a stop to Logan's dictates. She was willing to do whatever it took to get legal rights over Cody, but if things went on as they had so far, she could be looking at months of anger and frustration.

Cody started to climb onto the rocking horse, so she walked over to be close at hand as he tried it out. If she'd been an obedient little bride-to-be, she would have been in her room, putting a few things into her overnight bag for the trip to Vegas. The fact that she had at least a faint hope of slowing Logan down kept her where she was.

It wasn't long before she heard Logan's heavy boots coming down the hall from the main part of the house. His pace was relaxed but relentless, and she braced herself for an immediate dictate.

It was at least a small surprise when he merely walked in and stood watching as Cody happily rocked back and forth on the big rocking horse.

Logan said a pleasant, ''Looks like that old horse's gonna ride a few more miles,'' and he looked content enough to continue watching.

Claire didn't reply to that. Instead, she went about straightening the sheet on the baby bed before she spread up the little coverlet and walked over to one of the bookshelves to select a couple of Cody's stuffed animals to place in the bed.

The rhythmic sound of the rocking horse rails marked off the silence. Claire finished with the small tasks, then turned to watch Cody rock, her arms crossed over her chest in a way that suggested she'd be happy to stand there and watch him the entire day. As she suspected, Logan didn't put up with that indefinitely.

"For a female who said she doesn't like the silent treatment, you sure know how to dish it out."

She looked his way and gave her head a small shake. "Not at all."

Logan smiled a little, and that softened him immeasurably. There was a sudden ease between them, one that invited closeness, and that caught her off guard. His next words were almost fondly spoken in a low, rough voice.

"You're a hypocrite, Claire."

Claire studied his harsh face a moment. She could tell that the idea of her being a hypocrite amused him. It didn't amuse *her* though, and she was compelled to set him straight.

"It's hardly the same."

Now his dark gaze glittered with interest. "What's the difference?"

She couldn't have arranged a more perfect setup if she'd thought one up and written it out for him to recite.

"I'm dealing with a man who's made it abundantly clear that he doesn't care what I think or what I want. His agenda is apparently the be all and end all, so conversation between us will naturally be sparse."

A bit of his amusement flattened, though it was still there. "There'll be things we need to discuss."

"Such as?" she challenged, then shrugged. "'Do this,' or, 'Do that, or else,' don't require much more than a 'Yes, sir, right away, sir,' do they?"

She saw the flash of vexation, but she also sensed guilt—again—in the way Logan's dark gaze shifted slightly from hers before it came back. Now he was all arrogance again, which let her know she'd nicked his pride. And possibly shamed him into at least going through the motions.

"If you want to make a case for waiting, go ahead."

It was probably the only chance he'd give her to reason with him, and it was probably also obligatory. She didn't believe for a moment that he'd relent, or if he did, that he'd relent much, but she had to give this a try.

"I have a life, a modest business, an apartment, and belongings. It will take time to get everything sorted out and dealt with. This ranch is a long way from San Antonio, and I don't like jumping into a new life without properly settling things in the old one."

"I'll give you a hand once the ceremony's over."

Her frustration soared again, and she unfolded her arms. "Surely you understand how sudden this is? You and I could so easily come up with a shared custody agreement to raise Cody, without condemning us both to a—pardon me for being blunt, as well as accurate—a potentially hellish marriage. Marriage is a difficult prospect even when it's based on love and mutual respect."

Claire hesitated a moment, truly surprised that he'd kept silent through all that and appeared attentive and thoughtful. In fact,

Logan seemed amazingly mellow somehow, and she sensed some sort of agreement with the way she'd described their future. That encouraged her to continue on to make her full point.

''We aren't truly suited to each other anyway. I'm sure you realize by now that I'll be far more high maintenance and difficult to live with than a man like you might prefer.''

His dark brows went up in a wordless *Don't I know it* look. She tried not to take offense, though her next words were at least a tiny retaliation.

''And, if I might again be frank, you don't have quite the lifestyle and temperament of the kind of husband I had in mind. A shared custody arrangement could be ideal.''

Though Logan smiled faintly at that, she knew before he spoke that her reasoning hadn't made so much as a scratch on his determination to have his way.

''No dice.''

No dice! The man didn't waste any more time on tact and compromise than he did on basic good manners.

"And think about my friends," she went on doggedly. "They'll think I've either lost my mind or that I've been kidnapped. The first they'd never believe, so the second would cause them to involve the authorities."

An exaggeration, but certainly in keeping with her growing apprehension. The man was a brick wall, and the more she pushed against him, the more formidable he became.

He tilted his head back slightly in a way that was becoming familiar to her. But it wasn't done as if to look down at her from a slightly different perspective as she'd thought before, because it suddenly seemed as if he was looking down his nose at her. As if she was some lowly upstart that he looked down at that way to demonstrate not only his superiority, but also to signal his skepticism.

"We'll pay a visit to your friends while we pack up your things in San Antonio."

Claire felt her heart jump a little at that. Was this a reprieve? Her soft, ''When?'' sounded a little too eager and she regretted that the moment she heard it.

''After the ceremony.''

She made herself give a faint smile, though she didn't feel like smiling at all. ''You just made my point about discussions, so there's only one thing more I'd like you to consider before I give up completely.''

He stared down at her the longest moment, his expression stony though his dark eyes were alight with an amalgam of emotions: frustration, amusement, interest and possibly anger, though no one of those stood out more than the others.

Her overwhelming sense was that although she'd been almost too mouthy and challeng-ing, she'd not crossed the line that would make him take back his marriage demand and banish her from Cody's life. But then, her very boldness with him just now was because she'd sensed that the only thing that would make him take back his proposal was if she walked out on Cody.

Why she suddenly knew that was more a mix of subtle hints he'd given, rather than female intuition.

''What's that?''

She kept her voice low enough so Cody wouldn't hear specifics. ''If you're determined to do this today, then please reconsider taking Cody along. If you don't want him to go to Vegas, that might be okay. I could give my good friend a call and see if she could watch him for the day. Cody and her son are regular playmates, and we often baby-sit for each other. She owes me a couple of Saturday nights, so she might watch him today if she has no other plans.''

Claire felt some small release in the tension between them. As if her suggestion had provided Logan with the one compromise he might make.

''Call her.''

Claire resisted the urge to shake her head at yet another little dictate. At least it was a dictate she wholeheartedly agreed on, and it didn't escape her notice that because that idea would be better for Cody, he'd immediately agreed.

"I'd rather not call her before eight o'clock, if that's all right."

His solemn nod was not only permission, but probably meant that he'd already used up his quota of conversation for the day, although there was still plenty of time for him to work up at least enough "I do's" to get through the ceremony in Vegas.

That was the moment that Claire realized it would really happen. Today, at whatever time they arrived there and went through the formalities, she'd be married. This giant despot would be her husband.

"There's something I want clear," he said then. He moved to block her view of Cody, and his eyes were suddenly as cold as black ice. Claire read the warning in their depths and held her breath. His voice was a low rumble that was too indistinct for Cody to hear, but she caught every harsh nuance of his words.

''Don't ever try to come between me and the boy, or spoil him against this ranch.''

The utter grimness about him was so intimidating that Claire felt the shock wave of this dictate like a body slam.

Logan Pierce was such a strange, strange man, and there was a complexity to him that was as maddeningly impenetrable as it was suddenly intriguing.

Claire was certain then that for all Logan's awkwardness with Cody, the boy was of paramount importance to him. Perhaps the reason her insubordination hadn't seriously put him off was because he was willing to put up with it as long as it didn't interfere with his relationship with Cody.

Indeed, probably the only reason he put up with her at all and was determined to marry her was because Cody was so attached to her.

Clearly, the boy's happiness was a bigger priority for Logan than his own happiness was, and Claire liked him for that. Liked him a lot. At least he had that much going for him.

She gave a mute nod to let him know she understood this mandate, because nothing else was required. Though she'd meant to get free of Logan the moment she could, she suddenly wasn't sure it would be as easy as she'd thought. And it certainly wouldn't be easy on Cody at all, particularly once he settled in here and he and Logan began to bond.

How many months would it be before Logan allowed her to adopt Cody? And how long did the adoption process take? Cody was a loving child, and there was no doubt in her mind that if Logan was gentle with him and even half tried, that the little boy would soon love him. Cody would also naturally crave the man's approval, and because Logan would be his example, Cody's heart and life would mesh closely with his.

Claire's heart dropped at the realization. Oh, God. In light of Cody's future relationship with Logan, the reprieve and release she'd been looking forward to in a few months seemed impossible to contemplate now. And incredibly selfish. No shared custody arrangement could make up to Cody for a broken home. And it also wouldn't be fair to the boy if his home was a place of strife.

Feeling a little sick, Claire turned from Logan and gathered up enough of Cody's things to last him through the day before she went to her room to put a few of her own things in a bag. Claire stopped at one point to hold out her hands and noted with no surprise that they were shaking.

CHAPTER SEVEN

IT WAS just as well that they'd gone to Las Vegas and gotten married that day after a quick trip to Logan's attorney to sign the prenup. At least it was over with, and she wouldn't be tortured by the hope of somehow finding a way to avoid it. The marriage itself promised to be torture enough.

Ann had kept Cody for the day and everything had gone smoothly on their flights. Their quick trip to a Vegas mall for a proper dress went fine until Logan ushered her into a jewelers for a ring.

Though he hadn't been as particular about the white linen dress, white heels and handbag she'd chosen for the ceremony, he'd been adamant about the kind of rings he wanted her to have. His generosity in buying the elegant rings was surpassed only by his determination for her to submit to his selection of a set that fairly shouted her marital status.

The rings were indeed some of the most beautiful she'd ever seen, but the fact that they represented a marriage for Logan's convenience and one she saw as blackmail, rather than symbols of an eternal love pledge, made her feel guilty and pretentious. She'd be lucky if a thief didn't knock her on the head to steal them. Never having owned or worn anything this valuable would make wearing the costly rings an adjustment.

The requisite ceremony took place quickly at one of the many chapels in Vegas, but Claire was relieved that the one Logan picked was very nice. It bothered her that they hadn't been married by a minister, and since she was becoming more and more convinced that this was a marriage she might never be able to get out of without hurting Cody, she felt a deep need to have it blessed by clergy.

A marriage to Logan Pierce would need every bit of blessing it could get, particularly since it was already far more desperately in need of a miracle than the wedding at Cana had been.

Logan had worn a severe black suit that he'd taken along, then changed into in Vegas and worn for the trip back. He looked as handsome as sin in it, and with her white linen dress that matched the snowy white of his shirt, they were a startling visual depiction of purity and male menace.

Ann had been shocked by Claire's sudden plan to marry, but once they arrived back at her house late that afternoon to pick up Cody, Claire could tell that even Ann had fallen a little under the power of Logan's masculine appeal. And of course Logan's gallant manners and sincere invitation for Ann and her husband to bring little Tommy with them to the ranch for a weekend visit had delighted Ann.

As she and Claire gathered Cody's things from the playroom while Logan waited in the living room, Ann's slightly breathless, ''Oh my, you are *so* lucky, Claire,'' left Claire feeling blindsided by her friend's defection.

She didn't bother to set Ann straight, but she was aggravated. The rude autocrat Logan had been with her had managed in a mere few minutes that day to win over her friend with a polished manner and charm she'd never seen from him, much less suspected. The rat.

He had to know Ann would make a full report to their other friends, and the single ones were sure to be green with envy rather than concerned. And they were all too good-hearted and kind themselves to suspect they'd been taken in by a manipulator.

Claire endured Logan's gentlemanly she-nanigans in front of Ann and promised herself that she'd hold him to his polished manners from here on. At least the ceremony had given her some sense of security. The more people who found out about it, the more difficult it would be for Logan to toss her out if he was unhappy with her attitude.

She'd already gotten the message loud and clear that appearances were very important to him, so two could play the charm game with outsiders.

Outsiders. The word caught her a little off guard, and she was surprised at the sense of privacy and exclusivity she felt between her and Logan. They were husband and wife, and with Cody, they were a family, if only on paper. It was a little stunning to realize that everyone else had suddenly become outsiders.

On the other hand, the fact that she'd been blackmailed into this wasn't exactly something she wanted people to find out about, so that put her in the same fix regarding appearances as Logan was.

Thanks to Cody playing quietly with his cars in his car seat, the ride home was as quiet as it was long. Logan had draped his suit jacket over the back seat next to Cody, and discarded his tie. He seemed relaxed and satisfied, but that only served to make Claire even more aware of her growing tension.

It didn't help that when they arrived at the house and got out with Cody that Logan swept her up in his arms to carry her up the front walk to the door. The casual power of his big body gave her a feminine shiver that reminded her of the light kiss he'd given her in the chapel. It had been cool and chaste, but she'd sensed the dammed up sexual energy behind it.

She felt it in him now as the heat of his big body penetrated their clothes, and Claire was suddenly desperate to distract them both.

''This is so uncalled for,'' she said, trying to inject a ho-hum tone into her voice that was pure pretense. ''There's absolutely no one around to see this little act except Cody.''

As if he'd been cued, Cody piped up with a giggling, ''Mommy gets to be the baby!''

Logan chuckled at that, and the moment Claire felt the soft rumble in his chest, something very deep and feminine in her quaked with reaction. He gave her a sparkling look.

''Mommy wouldn't look like a baby if she'd put her arms around my neck like a grown-up woman.''

Reluctantly, oh so reluctantly, Claire shifted and put her arms around his neck. The little earthquake surged.

''Your wish is apparently my command,'' she told him.

The sparkling look flared. ''Then try a smile, Mrs. Pierce,'' he said gruffly, reminding her of what she'd said to him yesterday in Cody's room. He looked so smug as he parroted back her line to him. ''They look like this.''

His faint curve of lips widened arrogantly, and Claire was persuaded to smile in spite of herself. Logan was actually a little likable. And he must have decided to apply a bit of that masculine charm he'd worked on Ann. Claire tried mightily to keep him from guessing how much he affected her, but he did.

Suddenly everything about Logan was affecting her and Claire was shocked at herself.

When they reached the door, he easily turned the knob and gave it a shove to make it swing open. He carried her over the threshold then on into the foyer where he set her on her feet. The world tipped a little and Claire stepped back.

"We forgot our things," she said, feeling oddly shy with him after all that. And the sun seemed to be accelerating toward sunset. Now that they were home, all she could think about was the fact that her new husband expected her to sleep in the same bed as he did tonight.

And her body was fairly humming in the aftermath of being carried into the house. Cody's high voice was a welcome bit of normalcy.

"Carry *me!* Carry *me!*"

The big man turned toward him, and Claire saw Cody's eyes widen a little, as if his excitement had gotten ahead of his bashfulness. Logan chuckled and picked him up.

"How 'bout you and I bring in our things?"

Cody stuck a finger in his mouth and nodded, grinning as Logan carried him out. Claire watched the two of them, and some of her resentment toward Logan eased.

Cody indeed needed a man's influence, and for better or worse, Logan was that man. At least he'd wanted the boy badly enough to not only go through what he had with the courts, but also to marry the woman he considered important to his nephew. Now that he wasn't behaving as cold-bloodedly and heartlessly as before, Logan Pierce wasn't without potential, though Claire wished he'd gone about all this differently.

What would it have been like if he'd offered her a shared custody arrangement? What if he'd used those times to charm her as he had Ann that day? Claire was suddenly certain that if Logan had approached her differently, she might have been at least marginally attracted to him.

She'd planned to marry for love. It had never entered her mind to marry for any other reason. And yet here she was, married to an overbearing man she didn't love, who'd virtually taken over and run roughshod over her quiet, calmly ordered life.

Logan slung his suit jacket and his lightweight garment bag over his arm and gripped the handle of her small case in the same hand. Claire watched as he handed Cody the cloth bag, and felt a stirring in her heart. Side by side, man and boy came up the front walk and as they did, Logan leaned down enough to place his big hand on top of Cody's head.

Cody grinned and looked up at Logan, giggling. The very tall man looked down fondly. Claire saw the family resemblance between the two, and felt her heart warm a little more. Logan could be so good for Cody. If…

That ''if'' was the prelude to a long list of ''if only he would's'' that Claire couldn't let herself dwell on. It was too soon. Too soon to hope, too soon for marriage. Too soon to sleep together…

Her brain was stuck on that, and her thoughts were filled with schemes to avoid it. Since Logan would never allow her to do anything that would cause gossip about who slept where, she'd have to come up with something that would protect Logan's macho pride.

Which was ridiculous. It wasn't as if Elsa would be conducting surprise bed checks. Did Elsa know that Claire had essentially been a stranger to Logan until yesterday, and still was despite the mad trip to Vegas for the ceremony? If she did, what would the woman think of her for sleeping with Logan only a bit over twenty-four hours after her arrival at Pierce Ranch?

It was bad enough that she'd married a stranger for a reason she wouldn't disclose to others. Logan's wealth was more obvious than the fact that he had a nephew to raise.

Because Claire was anything but a sleep around sort, she had no wish to be seen as easy or without scruples. Or mercenary enough to sleep with a man right away. The fact that she'd married that man wouldn't make anything but a token difference to gossips.

"I wanna ride the pony, Unco."

Logan had barely closed the door before Cody came up with that one. Since it was evening, the little boy probably associated the time of day with the pony. It was a reminder that he'd loved the experience last night. It was also a reminder that the pony was a big attraction that Claire would have to monitor closely, whether Logan wanted her to or not.

"After supper," Logan said. "You'll need to wear long pants."

Claire knew Cody didn't quite understand what long pants were though he wore them most of the time. Claire referred to his clothes in more precise terms, such as jeans or overalls or slacks. All the little boy had paid attention to was the ''after supper'' part, but it was time for them all to change their clothes anyway, so she took over.

''Let's get your things put away.''

Logan followed them as Claire led the way through the house to Cody's room. Logan took her bag on to his room with his things, so she quickly got Cody dressed in a pair of jeans and a T-shirt before she stepped across the hall to the guest room to change into jeans of her own and a cotton shirt.

It had been obvious that Logan expected her to come to his room, since he'd taken her bag in there. Fortunately, she didn't need anything from it. She'd just finished and was in her bathroom brushing her hair when she heard Logan knock.

It was reassuring to know that he didn't feel entitled to just walk into her closed bedroom, so she hurried to the door as a sort of reward for that. Perhaps he'd rethought the whole idea of sharing a bed and he'd let her keep this room.

The moment she opened the door, she was faced with his stern, "Should I have Elsa move your things to my room?"

The man was dogged on the subject, but there was no sense triggering a showdown that might be overheard. "We'll discuss that after she's gone for the evening," Claire returned airily, and she glanced past him across the hall into Cody's room. "Where's Cody?"

Logan stared down watchfully at her a moment as if debating whether to press her or not, then said, "I told him to wash up for supper."

Now Claire noticed the sound of running water and winced. "He's good at turning on the faucet, but not at getting it turned off."

She stepped past Logan to walk across the hall and on into Cody's bedroom. The bathroom door was open, and she could already see a sheen of water on the tile floor. Now that she was closer, she could hear that the water was on full force.

Claire stepped gingerly into the bathroom and saw Cody standing on the stepstool, playing in the water with the soap. He'd put a washcloth in the sink, which slowed the drain only a bit less well than a plug.

The sink was now brim full of water that Cody splashed cheerfully in. Claire reached past him to turn off the faucet.

"The soap floats, Mommy," Cody reported guilelessly, demonstrating that by shoving the bar deep in the water then yanking his hand out of the way. The slosh he caused sent another wide ripple of water onto the counter that skated to the edge then over onto the floor. To Cody's delight, the soap popped up and bobbed jauntily on the surface.

Claire glanced into the mirror over the sink and caught Logan's look. His expression was a cross between surprise and horror, and she couldn't help but smile.

"Don't tell me. You only told him to wash his hands, and you're surprised because it seems like you only just now turned your back to walk across the hall.''

Logan's startled gaze came up to meet hers in the glass and Claire almost laughed at his dumbfounded expression. ''Weren't you a little boy once? Full of curiosity and mischief, and a tendency to try things out when Mommy was busy or looking the other way?''

It was a shock when Logan's dark gaze chilled and went flat, and his expression turned stony. His low voice was a gravelly rasp.

''Dry him off and come to supper.''

Stunned, Claire stared into the mirror, then glanced over to watch him go as Logan turned away and walked out of sight.

What had she said? Had she insulted him by asking ''Weren't you a little boy once?'' She hadn't meant to insult him at all!

If that wasn't it, then it must have been the mention of his ''mommy'' that had done it, because Logan had been anything but angry with Cody for playing in the sink and making a small mess.

As Claire dried Cody off then sopped up water from the counter, stepstool and floor, she decided it *had* been the mention of Logan's ''mommy'' that had caused his odd reaction. Perhaps she'd recently passed away and he was still grieving.

Though Logan was probably too macho to own up to feeling grief, she felt compelled to express some kind of condolence if the subject came up again.

Claire did her best to finish wringing out the towel she'd used before she draped it over the edge of the tub to dry awhile before she put it in the hamper. Cody had skipped off into his room, but from the sound of it, wasn't up to much except rocking on the rocking horse.

By the time the two of them reached the dining room, Elsa was just carrying in the food.

"Best wishes on your marriage, Mrs. Pierce," Elsa said pleasantly.

Claire smiled. "Thank you, Elsa. But please call me Claire. I'm not much for that kind of formality."

Elsa smiled back. "Sure thing."

"And by the way," Claire added as she helped Cody with his bib, "you're a fabulous cook, but if you ever need some help in the kitchen or around the house, I'll be more than happy to give you a hand. Though you might not notice it when I'm around Mr. Pierce, I can take orders."

Elsa lifted her dark brows and gave Claire a conspiratorial grin, though she didn't remark on that before she left the room.

When Claire turned back to the table, Logan was already towering nearby to seat her. The look on his grim face hadn't changed, but she saw the telling gleam in his eyes.

There, no doubt, because of what she'd just said to Elsa about taking orders from him. Because Claire recognized that gleam as amusement, she realized that she was suddenly able to read his stony face a little better and note more of the subtleties of his mood. She'd need every bit of advantage she could get if she was going to make this marriage a tolerable one for Cody's sake.

For the first time, Logan left the serving platter where it was to wait for grace to be said, but Claire could tell when they finished that he'd merely watched Cody and hadn't participated.

Claire made eye contact with him as he passed her the steak platter. "Eventually *someone* will notice that his closest male role model doesn't p-r-a-y before meals."

She knew Logan had caught her meaning, but she couldn't miss the fact that he didn't make any reassuring remark to let her know he meant to change that situation. Claire kept silent as she filled both her plate and Cody's.

If Logan didn't yet recall her specific requests yesterday about setting a good example in such things, she'd remind him later. Though it might seem trivial to others, Claire considered Logan's example as a man crucial, since Cody would grow up imitating him. Cody's development was all important to her and she'd proved that by obligating herself to a loveless marriage she'd probably have to live with the rest of her life. The least Logan could do was live up to the few things she'd specified.

It was certain Logan would insist on her living up to his specifications for a combination hostess/glamour girl/bronc rider, so the few things on her list hardly put any demands on him in exchange.

The silence during those first few minutes at the table felt anything but comfortable, so she introduced a natural topic.

"There are several things I'll need to take care of at home. I might as well get started tomorrow."

As she'd expected, that earned her Logan's complete attention. "I'll give you a hand. The sooner it's done the better."

Claire gave him a mild smile. "Cody and I can take care of it, though it'll take a few days. And I'd rather not drag him to and from San Antonio every day, so we'll stay over."

"No."

That one soft word carried the verbal power of a sledgehammer, which gave it an impact far out of proportion to her proposal.

Claire couldn't help the swift rise of temper, but she mentally reviewed all Logan's other dictates. So far, she'd gotten almost nowhere opposing them. If she was going to have any kind of a livable marriage with him, she'd have to solve these problems without creating a war zone. But how? Perhaps the first thing to do was get him to talk rather than dictate. She made a calm start.

"Will you elaborate a bit on your 'no' verdict?"

Logan stared at her a long moment. "I won't have a wife who lives in town. Or one who wears out the road between this ranch and San Antonio."

Claire was a little taken aback. What a radical conclusion to draw from so little! It struck her that there was a world of insecurity in what he'd said, and the perception was startling. Though she couldn't deny she'd hoped to have time away from him to adjust to all this, she truly did need to settle things in San Antonio. She was well aware that he'd oppose any sign that she was drawing things out unnecessarily, so she'd not likely get away with more than one or two attempts to do so.

But she couldn't allow him to be her jailer, whatever paranoia was afflicting him. Claire gave him a level look.

"I won't deny that I enjoy living in the city. I might enjoy living here too, but I'm not sure yet." Claire smiled stiffly. "However, I can guarantee that I'll resent every moment here and look for any opportunity to escape if I'm not free to come and go whenever I please."

Logan's gaze sharpened and she sensed his frustration with that. "You're anything but a prisoner."

"I appreciate knowing that," she said carefully, "but everything today and everything yesterday makes me feel...trapped."

She saw the flush that bloomed dully beneath his tanned cheekbones and suddenly knew she'd scored some sort of victory. As if he hadn't really thought too deeply about her feelings until that moment. The way his gaze flashed away from hers was a confirmation that she'd nicked his conscience.

The silence between them stretched and Claire wasn't certain what to say. After several moments more she realized nothing else needed to be said. At least *she* shouldn't say anything more. If there was any reason to hope Logan Pierce might turn out to be a halfway decent husband, he needed to provide her with a bit of solid proof.

"Wait till Monday," was all he said then, but it was enough to give her a spark of hope.

Particularly when she sneaked a glance to see that he was frowning down at his plate as he selected a forkful of food. Was he troubled over this or merely angry?

Cody managed to ease into the tension with a quiet, "When do we see the pony, Momma?"

Claire smiled at the eager little boy, noting that he'd only half finished his food. This was a prime opportunity for her to demonstrate a little good faith to Logan.

"You might ask your uncle Logan."

The boy looked Logan's way and Claire did, too, only to see him doing another intent search of her face. His mistrust of her was palpable. Was he only secure when she was challenging him? He'd evidently taken her suggestion to Cody as deference to him, but he seemed suspicious of it.

Would he understand that it was meant to help facilitate his relationship with the boy? And would he realize she was willing to do that because it was better for Cody? Or would he think she was doing it in order to get her way with something else later?

When Cody hadn't yet asked his uncle directly, she added a soft, "The pony belongs to your uncle."

Cody looked over at Logan and said a bashful, "I wanna see the pony."

Logan looked at the boy and his stony expression softened magically as he actually smiled. "Better finish that supper first," he said, nodding toward Cody's plate.

The boy reached eagerly for his small fork to comply, and Claire stared, touched by the gentle look that lingered in Logan's gaze as he watched Cody.

Whatever his shortcomings, the big man obviously felt strong affection for his brother's small son and the fact was, the man was too complex to either write off or fully accept.

Looking at him now, it was easy to believe Logan had enormous potential as a family man. And maybe even as a husband. Claire felt a small glow that smoothed away a significant number of her reservations, and she began to feel a bit more optimistic.

CHAPTER EIGHT

How had she ever thought Logan might have potential as a husband? Yes, their time at the corral with the pony had gone far better than the night before, and Cody had been just as reluctant to come back to the house as he'd been after his first ride on the pony.

But Logan was as bullheaded on the issue of where she slept on their wedding night as he'd been about getting married today. She might as well nickname him El Toro.

When they'd come back from the corrals, Claire had gone to her room to wash up while Cody went with Logan to the den. She'd discovered that all her things had vanished from the bathroom and closet. It didn't take a Sherlock Holmes to conclude that she'd find them in the master bedroom and bath.

Because Elsa had gone home, Claire's impending showdown with Logan promised to be a no-holds-barred shouting match after this. She thought about reclaiming her things right away but since Cody was still up, she prudently stayed in her room, pacing as she tried to calm down and think rationally about the ramifications before she rushed into battle.

The idea of sharing a bed this soon was ridiculous. Surely Logan knew that, because the man wasn't dense. She believed it was an issue of male pride as he'd said, rather than anything sexual, but it probably also had a lot to do with the fact that Logan Pierce was simply determined to have his way in everything. Because Claire was used to having things all *her* way, they were bound to have some horrendous clashes if neither of them was willing to compromise.

On the other hand, though she'd been strong-armed into this marriage, it was surprising how much she wanted it to succeed.

And yet she knew logically that success couldn't happen in a marriage full of one-upmanship and hostility.

Claire sat down on the edge of the bed in the guest room to give that serious thought. Picturing the man's earlier gentleness with Cody at the corrals made her feel warm toward him. It was obvious that Logan was capable of becoming just as wrapped up in Cody as she was, and of wholeheartedly parenting him in all the right ways, which could benefit Cody immeasurably.

Though Logan was awkward with the child and clearly didn't yet comprehend the maturity level of two-year-olds, it was clear he was trying to understand, trying to do the right things.

He'd glanced her way a couple of times as if to silently seek her guidance and approval, and that worked powerfully on her estimation of him as a man. It had also worked powerfully on her heart.

In truth, she was no longer quite as averse to Logan's dictate about tonight as she should have been. Part of that was because of those little glimpses of good in him. She couldn't allow sexual intimacy, but perhaps simply sharing his bed wouldn't be so terrible.

Confused by her seesawing attitude toward Logan but calmer now, Claire stood and left the guest room to see how Cody was doing with Logan. When she reached the den, she stood silently just outside the open door.

The scene on the carpet in front of the massive built-in shelves along one wall grabbed her by the heart. Logan lay on his side on the floor, with Cody kneeling opposite him. Between them was an impressive selection of small horses and cattle and mounted cowboys on other little horses, that obviously dated back to Logan's childhood.

A rough wooden chest she'd noticed before in the hall now sat open behind Logan, and it was crammed with boyish treasures that included little cars and trucks, Tinkertoys and Lincoln Logs. Several colorful rocks that might have been collected by Logan and his brother on some childhood adventure lay scattered beside the chest and placed in various spots among the herd of horses and cattle and cowboys they played with.

Logan was setting some plastic fence panels just beyond the cattle herd to form a big corral. Cody looked on intently, holding horses and cattle in both hands as he watched every move Logan made as if he were memorizing everything the man did.

''All right, little cowpoke,'' Logan said when he finished. ''Better get some of those cows herded to the pen.''

And then he moved one of the mounted cowboys toward a cow before he released the cowboy and shifted his hand to the cow to ''walk'' it toward the corral.

Cody caught on and thrust the cow he had in one hand to the floor to scoot it on the carpet into the corral. In his eagerness, he knocked over a fence panel, but Logan calmly righted it then reclaimed his mounted cowboy to guide the small piece toward another cow.

The boy found a little bowlegged cowboy of his own, painstakingly stuck it on the horse he held, then pushed his horse and cowboy along the carpet to keep up with Logan's. It was a beautiful demonstration of how to play with the old toys, and Cody's little face was beaming with both joy and excitement as he tried to imitate the play.

Claire managed to pull her gaze away from the child to focus on the man. Logan was so gentle, and he appeared just as intent on the toy scene on the floor as Cody was. Claire didn't want to say or do a thing to interrupt because the sight of all this was precious.

The jealousy she'd felt over Cody's small acceptances of Logan last night was gone. It wasn't just that marrying Logan had made her feel more secure, but that Logan hadn't set out to manipulate the boy with either the pony or these toys. Claire sensed that everything Logan was doing was not an effort to win the boy away from her and cut her out, but to find some way to genuinely connect with his nephew and build a good relationship.

She probably ought to step quietly out of sight and find something else to do for a while, but Claire couldn't seem to drag herself away.

Cody bumped down a row of fence panels and Logan again righted them as if it was merely part of the play. But then he stopped herding his cattle to simply watch Cody. There was a world of tenderness in Logan's dark eyes and his harsh face was remarkably relaxed.

It made Claire curious to know what he was thinking. Perhaps he was remembering his brother and something from their childhood. She wondered briefly how much Cody resembled Logan's brother, because he looked nothing like Farrah.

Claire began to realize that all her aggravations with Logan were evaporating as she stood there spying, and she liked him far more than she wanted to at this point.

She didn't truly know Logan, and yet she suddenly had the feeling that she knew the most important things about him simply because of his treatment of Cody. As bizarrely as all this had started, Claire felt far less opposed to Logan after watching him like this. Instinct told her that love and family were much more important to Logan than he'd ever admit.

And she no longer believed he didn't care about having love in his marriage. Judging by what she saw now, the real Logan Pierce wasn't a heartless, cold-blooded dictator who had to have everything his way. There was some other reason that a man like him used everything at his disposal to arrange and rearrange the world around him. People who were driven to do that had likely been through something so painful that everything they did was an effort to protect themselves from other disasters.

Was that why he'd blackmailed her into marriage? He'd said he didn't want the kind of wife who'd wear out the roads between here and San Antonio, which suggested some kind of extreme experience with that. Was it something to do with his mother? Some former lover or potential wife? And he was so uncertain of her that he wouldn't allow her to go to settle her business in San Antonio without him.

Claire was swiftly rethinking all this, and wondering even more how she should handle things between them after these little insights. She could be mistaken about everything, but what if she'd figured out at least a few things?

Perhaps she should have stepped quietly away, because it wasn't much longer before Cody stood up to brace his hands on Logan's hip and reach into the toy box behind him.

When he did, he caught sight of Claire, and immediately called out.

''Mommy! Come see! I gots horsies 'n' cowboys.''

Claire walked on into the room just as Logan glanced her way. Another faint flush crept along his cheekbones, as if she'd caught him doing something unmanly, so she fixed her gaze on Cody instead as the little boy stood up to run to her with his cowboy and horse.

''See, Mommy?'' he asked, barely giving her a chance to look at his new treasures before he turned to run back to the toys on the carpet.

Claire walked over, then got down on her knees to give Cody her complete attention as he showed her the little herd and picked out a horse and bowlegged cowboy for her to play with. She gamely put the small cowboy on the toy horse and posed it next to a couple cows that had fallen on their sides. She took a moment to right them, then glanced at Logan.

"Any orders from the trail boss?" she asked.

Logan gave her a sparkling look that she found quite appealing. "My top hand's got most of them rounded up. Except for your two cows." Logan nodded toward the ones she'd just straightened. "Better get 'em penned before dark."

Claire gave him a small salute. "Do I say, 'Sure thing, boss'?"

That got a faint smile out of him. "It's time for workin', not talkin'."

Claire moved one of the cows forward, then the other, then moved her mounted cowboy along behind them. As she walked the two feet to the corral on her knees to accomplish that, she had the attention of both males.

"Will someone please close the gate?" she asked as she walked her cows inside. Cody eagerly reached over to slide a fence panel into place to close the corral, but he knocked over three other panels in the process. Claire watched as he and Logan put the panels back into place.

Claire eased back. ''Well, now that the work's done for the night, it's time for little cowboys to get their bath done and their jammies on.''

It took Cody a moment to register what she'd said but when he did, he came up with an immediate, ''No, Momma, no baff.''

''You and Uncle Logan can play tomorrow, sweetheart.''

''No, Momma, I wanna play.''

Claire was familiar with the refusals and delays Cody regularly came up with at bedtime, but instead of handling them herself this time, she looked over at Logan. ''What do you think, Uncle Logan? Is it too early for little cowboys to get ready for bed?''

''It can't be too early for little cowboys, because it's about time for the big cowboys to do the same.''

His answer went completely over Cody's head, and Claire pointed discreetly at the little boy who was now hoarding several of the small pieces as if he was determined to keep playing.

''It probably needs to be said a little plainer, Uncle,'' she said and Logan sat up.

''Come on, son, let's get the toys put away.''

Cody glanced up and Claire watched the wordless byplay between the two. Logan's face was stern, though his dark eyes were alight. She held her breath while she waited to see what Cody would do.

As comfortable with Logan as Cody seemed to be, the big man was still a bit intimidating and Cody wasn't as certain of him as he was of her. The boy looked down at the cattle and horses he'd gathered to himself, then picked up a few and got to his feet to walk around Logan and put the small toys in the big box.

Claire was content to watch as they picked up the pieces and stowed them away. The pleasure she felt watching the little boy do his best to imitate the big man made her emotional.

It was so, so clear to her that Logan would be good for Cody. In fact, she realized now how tragic it might have been if Logan hadn't come into Cody's life. Being without a father would have left a huge gap in the child's upbringing, as well as in his heart, and Claire couldn't help that she was more than a little glad Logan had pursued custody.

Though she knew that left her with a husband she hadn't chosen and one she still wasn't certain she could have a happy future with, it was a fact that this marriage might turn out to be no better or worse in the long run than if she'd been the one to do the choosing.

As Claire got to her feet, she decided this was as good a time as any to involve Logan with the whole bedtime process.

"Would you like to see how baths get taken, Uncle Logan? And I'll bet someone would enjoy having you read the bedtime story."

The glimmer of surprise in Logan's dark eyes made her glad she'd thought of it. It was a goodwill gesture more than anything, but then, sharing everyday things with Logan, particularly where Cody was concerned, had to be the right thing to do.

And since she'd be sharing Logan's bed in another hour or so, it might help her get over some of her own jitters about that if they spent a little time doing something normal and low-key together.

"Might as well get started with those kind of things," he said before he reached down to pick Cody up then lift him higher to settle the wiggly boy on his wide shoulders.

Cody's giggles lasted well into the hall and Claire trailed behind, her stomach beginning to knot in earnest as she faced the waning minutes between now and bedtime.

*   *   *

Logan had allowed her to use the bathroom first, so she showered and dressed in the nightgown and robe she'd packed. The ivory-colored, thigh-length nightgown suddenly seemed daringly short, and the V of the neckline felt a little too deep and wide.

She wanted badly to wear her light robe over it to sleep in, but she didn't want to be ridiculous about this. She was twenty-four and an adult. She'd raised a child alone for the past two years, and she considered herself to be sensible and practical. She wasn't normally the nervous type, and yet she couldn't help feeling nervous now.

The important thing was to behave matter-of-factly. Logan was, no doubt, quite experienced sexually, but it would be a mistake to show any trace of nerves or to be skittish about this. Though sleeping in the same bed was rife with sexual possibilities, it was important to behave as if she wasn't even remotely expecting any of them to happen tonight.

A woman who showed neither expectancy nor cowardice sent a strong ''hands off'' message, and was much more likely to project the warning that a firm boundary was in place.

Claire had handled an occasional unwanted pass before, so the same principles should apply, though it was a fact that she'd never dealt with an unwanted pass while lying next to a man in bed.

Since Logan wasn't waiting nearby for his turn in the shower, Claire sat down on the edge of the mattress. Perhaps when it came right down to it tonight, Logan would let her off the hook. She was nervously toying with the ends of her robe belt as she considered stepping down the hall to check on Cody, when Logan walked into the bedroom.

He must have taken his shower in one of the other guest bathrooms, and the sight of him was arresting. She'd never seen his kind of bare maleness up close, and it was as unsettling as it was somehow thrilling to look at him.

The navy-blue pajama bottoms he wore barely registered because her gaze was fixed on the muscled expanse above them. His bare chest and torso, shoulder and arms looked as if they'd been carved from granite. It surprised her that his skin was tanned, but it was. His chest carried just the right amount of hair and she was glad of that because she didn't care for men with furry chests.

Her gaze drifted downward to his pajama bottoms, noted that the waist of them rested a little low on his hips, then traveled all the way down his long legs to feet that were big and almost perfectly sculpted. The man was a work of art, and she couldn't keep her gaze from tracking all the way back up to his face.

His expression was stony and solemn, as if he meant to be all business with her. But there was an intensity in his dark eyes that arrowed straight through her and made her incapable of moving.

If she'd had to make a guess, she'd say that look was a no-nonsense warning of some kind, or maybe one that established dominance without speaking a word. But it was also sexy as all get out, and Claire couldn't seem to help that her insides were quivering or that the heat that bloomed deep in her middle was suffusing her skin with warmth. It was a good thing she was sitting down because she wasn't certain her legs would have held her up. Then he spoke and she felt the warmth wash through her and go scorching.

"So you're gonna to do it."

It wasn't a question but a statement that told her plainly he'd expected otherwise. There was a spark of amusement in his gaze as he stared over at her. But he wasn't only staring into her eyes, he was staring at everything else, lingering on her bare knees for a moment before his gaze dropped to her toes. Her robe and nightgown felt distinctly transparent, and though her mouth was dry, she decided to take the small opening he'd unknowingly given her.

"I'd understood from you that Elsa does bed checks, that she's a compulsive and fluent gossip, and that your male ego couldn't survive the shame if everyone found out that your wife wouldn't sleep with you."

Claire lifted her brows as if to prompt his confirmation, but went on too quickly for him to give one. "So that's why I'm here, doing my humble best to uphold your reputation."

Something in his rugged face softened, as if he might have been bracing himself for some worse kind of resistance from her.

"Might as well climb in," he said, squashing her feeble hope that he'd change his mind.

The moment she'd dreaded had come, and Claire had to force herself to appear calm. She stood and turned toward the bed, dropping her gaze to the mattress as she untied the belt of her robe, striving to do it as casually and unselfconsciously as if she'd been alone in her bedroom at home.

Logan walked around the bed to his side and it was a little tougher to slip off her robe and drape it across the foot of the bed. Claire felt his dark gaze travel down her, and she braved the challenge to get into bed without making it look like she was desperate to keep the hem of her nightgown at a modest level. She almost couldn't take in a full breath until she could pull up the comforter.

The mattress dipped a little as Logan lay down beside her. She immediately felt the heat of his body and lay perfectly still, starting up at the ceiling as she gripped the edge of the covers.

Logan rolled toward her and suddenly his stony face loomed over hers. His fist was braced on the mattress by her hip, effectively trapping her. Whatever aftershave he'd used was subtle and musky and a little sweet. And he *had* used aftershave because she could see that he'd shaved.

He was so close that the heat pouring off his body made her skin prickle hotly, melting her insides, melting her bones, and he had yet to touch her at all.

His dark gaze seemed to be memorizing every feature of her flushed face, and she was helpless to do anything but stare back. His voice was a low rasp.

''I owe you an apology, Claire.''

If he'd wanted to surprise her, he'd got the job done. She searched his gaze for a clue to what he was talking about and if he was sincere about the word ''apology.'' It was on the tip of her tongue to ask him which thing he was apologizing for, since she could think of several, but she didn't.

''An apology?''

''When I said you needed more glamour. Something must have been wrong with my eyesight yesterday, because I can't see anything about the way you look that I'd want to change. I apologize.''

Claire was instantly suspicious, though she didn't detect any insincerity. He wasn't overly earnest and he sounded matter-of-fact. As if he was simply informing her that he'd corrected an errant opinion. But he was also letting her know that he wasn't so upset about his error that he meant to grovel and beg for her forgiveness. Just that he'd been mistaken and was apologizing.

"I appreciate that. Thank you." Claire couldn't help that she still felt suspicious of his motives. On the other hand, it would be a pretty shallow ploy—if it was a ploy—to get on her good side. She sensed he wasn't the kind of man to resort to flattery or shallow ploys. As he'd already proved, he was too blunt and determined to get his way for such namby-pamby methods.

She saw the glint in his dark eyes and knew right away that he was about to kiss her. Leery of that, she put up a hand as he started to lean down, and her fingers were suddenly pressing against his mouth.

Claire was surprised she'd actually done that, but she didn't want a kiss like the one last night. Not here, not now. And certainly not until she felt more comfortable sharing a bed with him.

"What if you just gave me a regular kiss good-night?" she asked, unable to keep the telling tremor out of her voice as she slipped her fingers from his lips. His rugged expression was going grim, and she felt the need to soften what his pride might take as a rejection. "S-something gentle and…sweet." She made herself give him a wry smile as she added, "A kiss that doesn't try to set the bed on fire."

It must have been the right thing to say because his expression gentled and his dark eyes glittered with interest. "You're runnin' scared, huh?" Claire's gaze shifted awkwardly from his.

"All of this has been so sudden, and I need time to adjust. You'd seemed to indicate that one of the reasons you chose me was because of my prudent lifestyle, so please understand that I can't instantly give you everything you said you wanted in a wife.''

She made herself look up at him and felt the hard blush that stung her cheeks. ''Yes, you showed me last night that you could get me to lose control, but I don't...want that so soon. At least not until we're more...used to each other. And we've rushed so much. Please, let's not rush everything.''

Logan smiled faintly. ''You talk a lot, Claire.''

''But you're listening, aren't you,'' she said, and it wasn't a question.

Logan's dark head descended slowly and Claire suddenly knew this kiss would be the gentle alternative she'd asked for. What she hadn't anticipated was how deeply it would affect her.

Tenderly, oh so very tenderly, Logan's cool, hard lips touched hers. If this had been another carnal, dominating kiss like the one last night, it would have done nothing more than arouse her lust and her heart might have remained aloof.

But the exquisite care he took with this one was breathtakingly sweet. She would never have imagined that Logan Pierce was capable of such a kiss, and Claire couldn't seem to help that her heart simply opened up.

Like the petals of a flower being coaxed by the warmth of the sun to open and unfurl, her heart trembled and began to grow warm and relax, and then to shyly reach out. Her fingers somehow imitated that trembling, shy reach for warmth, and she felt every tantalizing sensation as her fingertips touched his lean jaw, then pushed lightly and shakily into his hair.

A sparkling delight she'd never suspected was possible seemed to invade her and slowly drench her with pleasure, and she couldn't seem to help that her emotions were rising with something that felt a whole lot like joy.

As if for the very first time her heart was encountering something rare and wonderful and unique, coming close to touching something it had craved for a very long time. Whatever that something was, it suddenly seemed essential to her as a woman, and it somehow promised to be as fulfilling as it was desirable.

Too soon Logan's lips eased away, though they didn't go far. He trailed them lightly against her flushed cheek then on to her ear where he pressed a relaxed kiss before he pressed another just below her ear. His lips moved lazily down her neck before he stopped kissing her and his arms tightened fiercely around her for long, thundering moments.

He pulled one arm away to reach out and switch off the lamp before he slid it beneath her again. And then he moved onto his side, taking her with him to settle them face-to-face.

Claire rested snugly against him in the darkness, so deeply shaken and confused by that kiss that she couldn't speak. She was grateful he couldn't see her face, though she would have liked to see his and been able to read his reaction.

It was suddenly one of the most satisfying pleasures of her life to rest her hands against his warm, hard chest, feeling the solid rhythm of his heart beneath her palms as she savored the safe, protected feeling of being wrapped in his arms.

While she was luxuriating in every sensation and wondering what this all meant, Claire slowly drifted off to sleep, more at peace than she could ever remember being.

CHAPTER NINE

CLAIRE felt amazingly content that next morning. Until she realized Logan was lying on his back and that she was sprawled all over him. She cautiously lifted her head to see if he was still asleep, but held back her sigh of relief while she carefully moved off him and got out of bed. She quickly collected her clothes then rushed into the master bathroom to get dressed for the day.

It was just after 5:00 a.m. Since she didn't know how early Logan normally got up, she wanted to take care of her makeup and hair before he was awake. Finished in record time, she cleared her things from the counter, then quietly opened the door and tiptoed out into the bedroom. Logan's rough voice startled her.

"You won't get away with that tomorrow," he told her, and Claire glanced toward the big bed. Logan was sitting up with his back resting against the headboard.

Her soft, "Good morning," helped her avoid making a comeback. "Shall I bring your coffee?"

"I'd appreciate that," he said, then gave her a slow, sexy smile. "Just bring it right on into the bathroom when you get back."

Yikes! The man was more dedicated to his mission than ever, so Claire rushed out into the hall then on into the kitchen. Since she was just as dedicated to her mission—to put the brakes on things—she didn't exactly rush back with his coffee like an obedient little wife.

It was then that she realized how different she felt about Logan now. After that sweet kiss last night, he'd been a gentleman. Her skin still tingled at the memory of being wrapped in his strong arms all night. Heaven help her, her body had loved the feeling of lying against him, and now her heart was re-markably changed.

Not rushing back to take his coffee to him quickly began to feel like a mistake. In the end, the odd excitement of wanting to please the strange and interesting creature she'd married lured her back to the master bedroom and across the carpet to the open door of the master bathroom.

To her relief, Logan had dressed in his jeans and boots, though the jeans' snap was open and he wore no shirt. He'd just lathered his face for a much-needed shave—his jaw had been rough with beard stubble—and he was about to lift the razor to make the first stroke. She saw the glitter in his eyes as his gaze met hers in the mirror.

"I'd rather start my coffee before I shave," he said, but it was more a comment than a criticism.

Claire gave a small shrug. "If you're a be-nevolent dictator today, my timing might im-prove tomorrow." She walked over to set his coffee on the counter. He turned his head to look down at her.

"How good are you with a razor?"

The question startled her. It was an invitation she couldn't have imagined him making, and she wasn't sure how to take it. Except that her heart had accelerated a little.

"I've never shaved a man before, but..." she hesitated to turn him down because there was something appealing about the way he was looking at her. Something almost playful, so she replied in kind.

"If you're willing to put your life in my hands, I won't hesitate to make the most of the opportunity," she said, then gave him an innocent smile.

The glitter in his dark eyes intensified. "I can tell you'll never be a dull wife."

"Was that what you thought you'd get?"

"Yes, ma'am." His low drawl was as sexy as the faint smile that softened the hard slash of his mouth.

Claire couldn't help that her insides quivered a little, because he didn't seem unhappy about that. Still, she hoped he'd make it a little plainer.

"You must be *so* disappointed."

Logan held out the razor to her. "I'm anything but disappointed, Claire."

Leery of shaving him but liking this too much to refuse, Claire gamely took the handle. Fortunately for him, the razor was the safer kind with a disposable blade.

"You'll need to sit down or my arms will get too tired."

Logan moved over to close the lid on the mode and sit. Claire went along and tried cide where to start.

y advice or instructions?"

rinned a little. "You complain about ossed around by a tyrant, but now sking for advice?"

s. Guilty." Claire made herself go "Don't talk, and whatever you do, ve."

She carefully positioned the razor against his jaw and lightly drew it up, feeling the blade scrape away the lathered beard stubble.

"Ah, this is easy," she commented after she'd worked awhile, rinsing the foam from the razor periodically. "Just sit you down somewhere, order you not to talk and not to move, and then enjoy the novelty of having you at my mercy with a sharp object in my hand. I could get used to this."

Logan didn't reply, but through the whole process, she could feel his gaze on her face and then down the front of her.

Her knee often brushed his thigh, and she couldn't help but be affected by that standing so close.

And the fact that she had to use hand to angle his head this way while she worked, and that he'd resp her so easily, was also affecting he just her light touch alon was enoug trol a very dangerous and powerful

The notion stirred some need for feminine power that she'd not realized she had.

It was a surprising disappointment to finish the last stroke, and she moved away to rinse the razor before she wet a washcloth under the faucet and turned back to him. It took only a few moments to wipe away the last traces of shavi   foam from his face, but the small task seemed even more intimate than shaving him had been.

To distract them both, she commented, ''Little boys' faces, big boys' faces. Both need a lot of maintenance. So what are your plans for the day, boss?''

con.
to de   a took the washcloth from her fingers
''An ed it toward the counter as he stood
He   re took a prudent step back.
being   pend the day in bed with my wife.''
you're a gave him   o-nonsense shake of
''Ood as he rea   for his coffee and fi-
serious. a sip. ''S   e you won't be getting
don't m what's Pla

He set the cup on the counter. "To get you on a horse."

Claire rolled her eyes and walked out of the big bathroom into the bedroom. "How about I just jump off a cliff or throw myself off the barn roof?" she asked as she glanced briefly over her shoulder to see him follow her out. "That way, we can have the same result without pestering one of your horses."

Logan plucked his shirt off the doorknob to the walk-in closet and started to put it on. "You're that chicken, huh?"

Claire took a few moments to fluff their pillows before she efficiently made the bed. He was teasing her about being a chicken, and since she couldn't detect scorn for her fear, she decided that now was as good a time as any to tell him the story.

"I was ten years old when I rode one of my uncle's horses. I'd probably made it once around the pasture before the horse bucked me off, broke my wrist, then stepped on me before I could get off the ground."

She walked around the bed to Logan's side and spread up the top sheet and comforter. "After I was on my feet, the horse my cousin was riding bit me on the shoulder." She finished and turned slightly to point to a place on the back of her shoulder under her shirt. "I still have the scar. I'm a complete chicken, except I don't have feathers and I don't lay eggs."

Claire watched his stern face while he buttoned his shirt. "You need a rooster for that."

Relieved things were still light between them, she said, "Good point, but since I don't seem to be able to help it, it's a waste of time to bother. I tried a couple of other times to ride after the cast came off. My uncle took it all so seriously that he forced me to get on a horse, and yelled at me. Cussed, too. I promptly lost my lunch, along with whatever dignity or hope I had left."

She laced her fingers together in front of her as he finished buttoning his shirt and began to briskly tuck the tail into his jeans. He'd not commented on anything so far, so she was persuaded to confess the rest. But as much to caution him about the futility of pushing her to try again as anything else.

"I became the laughingstock of that part of the family and lived through it, so I'm immune to being shamed or coerced or cussed into trying again."

Logan silently finished with his shirt. He seemed to have taken what she'd said seriously, but what amazed her was that he appeared to accept that she couldn't be pressured into another try. Relieved, she walked around the bed and stopped to wait for him before she started for the hall.

He met her gaze somberly. "You might want to reconsider sometime, because you have a little boy now. Think how you'll feel when his life revolves around horses and riding, and you can never go along."

She only had a half second to register the pleasure of his "You might want to" beginning before the rest of his words struck her heart like a soft punch. With just a few quiet words he'd managed to ensure that she wouldn't be able to ignore her fear of riding and just go on happily afoot. Her voice was soft and a little choked.

''Just when I begin to think you might not be the quite manipulative cretin you started out to be, you manage to give me fresh evidence.''

There'd been no real fire in the words that were more a signal of impending surrender than criticism. Logan seemed to know that, and he moved close to gently take her hands.

The part of her heart that wasn't aching over the thought of Cody's interests and hers dividing at some point was surprised by the comforting gesture.

''It'll be different this time, Claire.''

She looked up at him, sick that she had absolutely no confidence in that. She'd been afraid of riding too long. ''And if it's not?''

''You'll have a choice at every step.''

Claire gave him a doubtful smile. "Will I?"

His face was still somber. "You have my word."

Claire was deeply touched by that, by this, and as he leaned down, her eyes drifted closed. It was another sweet, sweet kiss, and her heart responded much the same way as it had last night.

Oh how she hoped this was the beginning of good things for this marriage! If she could somehow survive Plan B without being killed or going catatonic, it might be a sign of more good things to come. Claire knew already that mastering her fear would also enhance her relationship with her husband, and she wanted that now. Wanted it a lot.

Logan drew back slightly. "Think the boy's awake yet?"

Grateful for the change of subject, her soft, "Probably," was barely a whisper.

If she hadn't been so deeply worried about Logan's plan to take her riding and her certainty of both trauma and failure, Claire might have realized how far her heart had gone toward falling in love with him.

Claire couldn't get down more than three bites of toast at breakfast. After she'd made sure Cody and Elsa would do well together, she joined Logan at the back door. She suffered being fit with a Stetson and a pair of western books that were kept on hand for guests, then walked out with her solemn husband to meet her fate.

To her surprise, they got into one of the ranch pickups and drove away from the headquarters. Too preoccupied with worry and a mental litany of desperate little clichés along the lines of "What won't kill you will cure you," and the old, "I am woman, hear me roar," Claire didn't pay much attention to the panorama of range land around them.

When Logan drove toward a stand of abandoned wood rail corrals, she noted the corrals weren't quite abandoned. Two saddle horses and Cody's pony were tethered in one of the pens. It didn't take much to figure out why the pony was there.

"Oh, Logan," she breathed out, then gave a helpless chuckle. "No wonder you brought me to the back forty."

Clearly, he meant to start her out on the pony, and her pride squirmed. She felt about two inches high—which was just as well because the pony was small.

But Logan would be the only human witness, and at least she had some confidence that he'd never repeat what he saw here today. Male pride alone ensured that. After all, he'd have to be able to hold his head up among the macho set, so he could hardly blab the news that he'd used a pony to help his wife get over her fear of riding.

Resigned to the excruciating embarrassment but mightily relieved because at least she couldn't fall far if the pony threw her off, Claire got out of the pickup and walked with Logan into the pen.

It took him only a moment to slip off the pony's halter and put a pony-sized bridle on its head. He passed her the reins and she made herself take them.

''You can begin by handling him from the ground,'' Logan said, then instructed her in the basics, as if she was no older than Cody. It was a small reprieve—after all, she couldn't miss the significance of the two saddled horses nearby—but she appreciated the chance to become a little more comfortable with the pony before she actually had to ride him.

Polite and well-trained, the pony complied with everything Logan had her do, from leading it around to removing its bridle then putting it back on. She actually managed to get the knack of lifting the pony's feet. Logan apparently could tell the moment she felt at ease.

''Lead him over here, and I'll hold him while you get on.''

Claire turned toward him and brought the pony over. ''Bareback?''

''The only saddle that fits him is a kid saddle. Too small for you.''

''You're sure I won't hurt him?''

''He's big enough to carry you.''

Of course he would be. Logan knew horses, so he must be right, and the muscular pony's back was almost as high as her waist. Claire handed over the reins. Not quite so nervous, she faced the pony's side.

While she was trying to figure out how to get on the sleek back, Logan stepped over and caught her waist to lift her up. He'd startled her, and Claire spent those first few seconds trying to get her balance.

And then Logan led the pony much as he had with Cody. He periodically had her dismount then get back on by herself, and she quickly figured out how to do both with some semblance of grace. Logan took a moment to explain neck-reining, then turned over control and stepped away to coach her as she rode around the corral solo.

Absurdly thrilled, Claire felt like crowing as Cody had the first time Logan had taken him riding. From there, it was easier for Logan to talk her into mounting one of the big horses. He followed the same procedure, first leading the horse then handing her the reins.

Nervous but not as terrified as before, she cautiously rode around the corral, following his commands to switch directions, stop and back up. The huge horse calmly obeyed her every signal and gradually she felt more at ease.

Too soon for her jittery stomach, Logan put the pony on a lead rope, mounted the other horse, and led the way as he opened the gate and kept watch as Claire rode along to follow him out.

Her insides were still a mass of quivering jelly, but she was actually riding a horse! The ground didn't look so far down after a while, and the animal seemed willing to plod harmlessly along under her cautious control.

Leery of claiming success prematurely, Claire kept silent until they'd reached the stable at the headquarters. Flushed with victory, Claire started to dismount, got a leg cramp, then began to slide helplessly down the side of the horse. Logan caught her waist to slow her descent, but her knees buckled when her feet touched the ground. If he hadn't kept hold of her, she'd have ended up in the dirt.

"Let's walk you around," he said, and Claire clung to his arm until she could walk on her own. "That won't happen once your legs get some muscle on them," he remarked.

"That's good," she said and let go of his arm. They handed off their horses to a stable hand and started for the house.

Claire couldn't get the wide smile off her face, and she knew she must look like a grinning fool.

"I can't believe it, Logan. I actually rode a horse. A really, really big one."

Logan's eyes twinkled as he smiled over at her. "You're on your way."

Claire's excitement animated her. "I never thought it could happen—this is so unbelievable! I was embarrassed about the pony, but you were right to have me ride him first." She grabbed his arm with both her hands and gave it a shake, absurdly thrilled over the accomplishment.

"I take back every mean thing I ever thought about you. I can't believe it was so easy! *You* made it easy—you're a genius. You got me to ride a horse and I actually stayed on! I can't explain what it means to me to be able to do that. It's because of you, Logan, *only* because of you."

She was so excited that she couldn't seem to help that she stopped and tugged on his arm to prompt him to lean down.

"You are the most wonderful man—I *so* underestimated you." It was in her heart to give him a "thank you" kiss. Logan had started to oblige when a feminine voice intruded and startled them both.

"I can't believe Logan Pierce would marry a city girl who couldn't ride a horse before this morning."

Claire jerked her head in the direction of the voice and felt her face go fiery as she realized she'd been so completely oblivious to the woman's approach that she'd babbled out what she'd hoped to keep secret from the rest of the world.

The gorgeous brunette stood with her hands on her svelte hips, and she looked as at home in her Stetson, work clothes and boots as she would have in a sequined gown at a ball. Instinct told Claire that this woman was an expert with everything to do with horses and ranch life.

She was probably also an expert in sequined gowns and ballrooms. Claire could almost see the word "debutante" in the green eyes that looked her over with enough pity in their depths to make her feel like an idiot.

Not used to bearing that kind of attitude with any kind of grace but not yet certain what Logan's relationship with the woman was, Claire made herself give a stiff, polite smile.

"Hello, my name is Claire," she said as she recovered her confidence and stepped forward to offer her hand to the woman.

Logan finished the introduction. "And this is Kiki Lynch. She's one of our neighbors."

The woman put out her hand as if she was only reluctantly allowing the gesture. She let go of Claire's fingers almost before their hands made full contact, and then simply dismissed Claire's presence by addressing Logan.

"When you decide to do something, you sure keep it to yourself."

"No need to advertise."

There was a hint of displeasure in Logan's low voice that the woman appeared untroubled by, but the shorthand exchange indicated a familiarity that Claire couldn't mistake.

''Well, bring her along Saturday after next, and let folks get a look at her.''

As if she needed another look herself, Kiki's green eyes flicked over Claire, and again Claire saw the trace of pity. She felt compelled to say something.

''What happens Saturday after next?''

''Mama and Daddy are havin' a barbecue to celebrate my birthday.''

''Happy birthday.''

Kiki gave a wave of her hand. ''It's not for three more weeks,'' she said, effectively cutting Claire out as she stepped between her and Logan to take his arm as if she did it regularly.

''You've been keepin' me in suspense for a whole month, darlin', so now you don't get a choice. You'll want to introduce Carla around, and there's no better place to do it than in a crowd.''

Claire stared in amazement as Kiki slathered on the charm in a bid to not only persuade Logan to show up, but the woman was squeezing then stroking his arm as if making love to it. Logan's stony expression didn't change a whit and Claire felt a burst of hilarity. Kiki's ploy to trivialize her by referring to her as Carla instead of Claire was hardly original, and that made it difficult to keep a straight face.

On the other hand, Logan was keeping a straight enough face for both of them so Claire decided to enjoy this. After all, nothing could truly spoil the accomplishment of that morning, and Claire was content to listen to Kiki wheedle and tease as they all walked along.

CHAPTER TEN

OBVIOUSLY, Kiki Lynch must have had a marital hope or two of her own. Casual friends just didn't behave as she was, but Claire felt surprisingly secure about Logan. He apparently could have married Kiki, who clearly felt some sort of entitlement to him, anytime he'd wanted to. But he must not have wanted to. Besides, Logan had to know already that his new wife didn't have a personality that would tolerate even a hint of infidelity.

Claire was just trying to picture the kind of people who would name their daughter Kiki, when they reached the house and walked into the kitchen. Claire hung her Stetson on the wall peg and glanced around for Cody.

He was playing with an assortment of little trucks and cars under the kitchen table at the end of the big kitchen while Elsa hand-mixed what looked like cake batter at the counter. The little boy's excitement to see them was curtailed by the presence of the tall brunette. Ever bashful, he stayed under the table.

Kiki hadn't noticed him yet so Claire walked over to the table and bent down. Cody crawled out and she caught him up in a hug.

"Hello, sweetie, give me a kiss." Though Claire had kept her voice low, picking the child up had got Kiki's attention.

"That's not your boy, is it?"

Kiki had asked bluntly, as if she was entitled to have answers to anything she wanted to know.

"Why yes, he is," Claire answered, "in every way that matters. Logan and I will be adopting him soon. And his name is Cody."

"He's Cliff's boy," Logan said, and Claire couldn't tell if he approved or disapproved of her declaration about adoption until he added, "Claire and I will raise him like our own."

Something in Claire relaxed. It was one thing for Logan to propose that privately, and to even sign a prenup few would ever see or know about. But now that he'd declared it publicly, she felt more reassured.

Besides, it didn't take deep instinct to know that through Kiki everyone in Texas would know about it by noon, and public knowledge might prompt Logan to hurry the adoption process along.

Not that she didn't think he'd come through, and not that she hadn't already decided it was in Cody's best interests for her to stay married to Logan, but she wanted them to go forward with the adoption soon because it would settle something important between them. Or at least it would settle one important thing.

Claire's sudden craving to settle all the important things between them was surprisingly sharp.

Kiki's bald, ''I wondered why he looked like Logan,'' said a lot about Kiki's first impression. And the faint look of irritation on her beautiful face as much as announced that she might have hoped Logan's sudden marriage was more because of an out-of-wedlock child than because he'd been smitten.

Though Kiki wasn't completely mistaken—this *had* been a marriage for the sake of a child—Claire suddenly hoped no one would ever know the truth. But she didn't know enough about Kiki's relationship with Logan to predict whether he would ever confide it to the woman.

On the other hand, common sense suggested that his failure to confide to Kiki his plans to marry—though he must have been planning it for a while—was probably the biggest clue that Kiki would never know the whole story.

Claire could tell by the way the woman's gaze narrowed that she wanted far more information that she was getting, so Claire looked over at Logan as the awkward silence stretched.

His voice was low. "Cody's mama passed away. Claire was taking care of the boy, and one thing led to another."

Claire couldn't help smiling. It was the complete truth, but most people would assume that the one thing that led to another was love. A court battle that ended in blackmail would never enter most folks' minds, so no one would be the wiser. And Claire didn't want anyone to know the real circumstances anyway, so what Logan had said covered it nicely.

Kiki seemed to lose interest right away, which was hardly a surprise. She'd obviously come over to find out what was going on, and now that she thought she knew, she might be eager to spread the news. And there was always the chance that the idea of Logan marrying for love had squashed whatever romantic hopes the woman had, so she might be just as eager to come to grips with that in private.

As Logan walked Kiki to the front door, Claire trailed along carrying Cody. She hadn't heard Logan agree to go to the barbecue and apparently Kiki had been too distracted by Cody and the love affair Logan had hinted at to remember that the barbecue had been part of her excuse to show up here so early.

Logan had just closed the door behind their nosy neighbor when he turned to Claire and plucked Cody out of her arms to stand him on the floor. He took off his Stetson and tossed it to the table in the entryway.

''We were interrupted just before I was about to be rewarded for being wonderful and misunderstood, and whatever other qualities you were about to name.''

Claire adored the way his eyes glittered as he said that and his stern mouth curved with a male arrogance that suggested he was more than ready to bask in the glow of whatever praise he might have coming. And the curve of his handsome mouth showed he also expected the kiss he'd missed getting on the way to the house.

"Oh my. A little praise certainly went to your head, didn't it?" Claire crooked her finger to get him to bend down a little. He obliged, and she reached up to pull him closer.

"In case I didn't make it plain enough earlier, I'm so, *so* thrilled about what you did for me this morning," she said, then gave him a cheeky grin. "You're not quite the horrendous jerk I was afraid you were, so I want to give you a big kiss."

Claire urged him down that last couple of inches, but instead of kissing his mouth, she landed a big kiss on his lean cheek then drew back playfully to wait for his reaction.

Logan's arms came around her and briefly lifted her off her feet, but it was Claire who kissed him. The kiss immediately became something far too fiery to go unnoticed by the little boy who started hollering and clapping his hands.

''Mommy's kissing Unco! Mommy's kissing Unco!''

Logan's response was to break off the kiss then lean down and catch up the child. Cody giggled as Logan sandwiched him between them, but when Claire supplied a flurry of kisses to the little boy's face, he began to shriek with happy laughter.

The rest of the day seemed a portent of good things to come. They took Cody with them as Logan drove them around the ranch, then stayed in during the heat of the day. While Cody had his nap, Logan retreated to the den to do paperwork. Elsa showed Claire where things were in the kitchen and pantry to prepare for her days off, since Claire would do the cooking on Sunday.

That evening after Cody was bathed and read to and put to bed, Claire got out Cody's baby book and the journal she'd kept. Logan seemed to enjoy looking at them, and that pleased her.

Later, they'd gone to bed, and Claire was relieved that things were still restrained between them. The kisses were a little less sweet and a bit more carnal, but nothing more happened and she again had the unexpected pleasure of lying next to him.

That next day they tried one of the churches in the area, and afterward, Logan decided they might as well go on to San Antonio so they'd be ready to deal with settling her job on Monday.

It was a relief that Logan couldn't spend enough time in San Antonio this week to both deal with her work and take care of everything in her apartment. For now, they'd pack up as many personal things as they could to take to the ranch, but it was reassuring to Claire to know she'd have some time to adjust to what would be yet another radical change in her life.

Though Claire's apartment was hardly a something out of a decorating magazine, it was tasteful and attractive and pleasant. Once they'd got to San Antonio and carried in the things they'd brought along, Logan had walked through looking everything over.

Claire had also been looking around, thinking about how long the place had been home, and how much she'd enjoyed the modest but interesting things she'd acquired and how much she hated to give them up.

Very few of the things she'd been able to afford would look right in Logan's expensively furnished home, but Claire was deeply sentimental about it all. And getting rid of everything suddenly wouldn't have allowed her much time to come to terms with it.

Logan came into her bedroom as she was standing in front of the closet, contemplating the job ahead of her. She looked his way as he picked up a little knickknack angel on her dresser. He studied the delicate face a moment then set it down and glanced around the room.

It was a feminine room, with small roses trailing on the wallpaper, and a white bedspread with embroidered roses on the center and around the edges.

''I'll go out and get some boxes while you get started,'' he said. ''If there's more than we can get into the SUV, we'll look into hiring a trailer.''

Later when Logan returned with a thick stack of flattened boxes, they set to work, assembling the boxes then filling them with things out of closets and drawers until it was time for Claire to cook supper.

On Monday and Tuesday, Claire took care of her work, giving notice to the doctors' offices she did transcription work for. Two of her friends from church, who also did medical transcriptions, were able to divide her clients between them, and the offices were satisfied with the new arrangement. Logan reserved a trailer for the belongings they'd be taking back to the ranch on Wednesday.

Over that two days, Claire felt their relationship deepen. Cody thrived on Logan's attention and gentle discipline. Claire felt increasingly comfortable and began to truly enjoy being married to him.

Nights caused the only real tension between them, and all of the tension was sexual. On their first night in San Antonio they'd come precariously close to intimacy, but Claire's unspoken wariness of that caused Logan to confine things to a few kisses, both day and night. Claire had grown impatient with his restraint, and that surprised her.

But then, the heartless dictator Logan had been seemed to have faded away leaving in his place a good man with a gentle touch and a sense of humor.

The fact that she'd fallen completely in love with this new man had become stunningly evident as time had gone on, and Claire was still a little in shock. The runaway train that was their marriage had pulled into that particular station hundreds of miles sooner than she ever would have guessed it could, and she'd spent most of that time trying to talk herself out of it.

And yet she couldn't seem to help it. Going by how he was with Cody and also with her, Logan Pierce had more wonderful instincts and qualities than he even knew about. It was a distinct pleasure to watch each one of them drawn into the open in such a short space of time. She couldn't have resisted loving him now if she'd tried.

Her brain was still stunned by how suddenly it had happened. After all, they'd only been together a hectic six days, and only a day less than that as husband and wife. And yet falling in love with Logan this quickly felt natural and right.

Loving him so soon was easily the biggest risk she'd ever taken, and all she could do now was hope for the best. On the other hand, how long did it take for love to happen? Wasn't there usually one significant moment when the heart recognized something special and made its decision?

It had just happened far sooner than Claire had ever dreamed it could. And as Logan had grown more companionable than domineering, Claire's natural optimism seemed to enable her to see past the inevitable bumpy spots ahead to the time when the road would even out and things would go even more smoothly between them.

Their last night in San Antonio, they settled in front of the television after supper while Cody watched a video. They gave Cody his bath and let him sit up with them playing while they watched an old Humphrey Bogart film on cable.

By the time Logan carried the soundly sleeping boy to bed, Claire was more than ready for a shower and some sleep. All went well as they took turns in the bathroom, and once they were settled in Claire's bed and the light was off, Logan leaned over to kiss her.

Before the kiss could get out of control, Claire pressed against his chest and he eased back.

"I appreciate that you're giving me time to let go of this apartment," she said quietly. "I'm not sure I completely believe that you have to get back to the ranch tomorrow, and it's sweet of you to give me time to adjust to the idea of giving up this place."

Logan's low voice had an appealing gruffness. "Are you one of those folks who are happy all the time and only see good things in others?"

Claire giggled a little. "Hardly. People like that are annoying. In fact, I had quite a low opinion of you at first, as you know. But you're a big rough, tough fake, Mr. Pierce. I'm not sure why you work so hard to hide your gentle side. You've a very kind and thoughtful man when you take off your crown and ask rather than issue decrees."

"You *are* a Pollyanna." That had come out in a growl. "Either that or you're working me."

Claire clearly heard the mistrust in that and was disappointed. She'd relaxed so much with him these past few days, and he'd seemed to take her at her word. She'd thought her forthrightness had earned as much trust from him as his gallant treatment had earned from her, so she couldn't allow him to mistake this.

"Perhaps I need to elaborate a little," she said. "I didn't want this marriage, and I've been worried about it. I might worry about it again tomorrow or next week, but I like what's happened the past few days. It all seems good to me. Very good. Since we're married, we might as well be happy. For Cody's sake first, but also for us."

Logan didn't say anything to that, and she again got a fleeting sense of mistrust. But then he covered the back of her hand with his to lift it. Claire couldn't help the warm shiver when he pressed a lingering kiss into her palm. She must have been mistaken about the mistrust.

And then his tenderness struck her as she felt him lean down and softly, so softly, kiss her. His lips were expert, very expert. His kiss was different tonight, and Claire was so suddenly overwhelmed by the sensual magic of his lips and then his hands, that her brain ceased to function rationally.

She couldn't seem to find the will to resist him this time, or to even temper her response, and all too soon she was caught up in the sensual give and take of all the things he lavished on her. More of that, and she became an almost wholly physical creature, dominated by sensation and instinct and the relentlessly advancing sexual power of a man who knew exactly what to do. Any reserve she'd had in the past and any scruples against full intimacy, made brief, fleeting impressions before they fell, one by one, like a row of dominoes.

Her initial misgivings and worries and shocks over a marriage that had started as poorly as this one, were so absent now it was as if they'd never existed. Female was bonding with male at a level so primal that everything else had become little more than dry leaves blown away by a warm spring wind.

From there, it was a short distance to the next things. Her nightgown somehow vanished and was forgotten about, and her body went wild as warm flesh met warm flesh. At some point, her awareness of anything but her body and his drifted out of her consciousness, and they ceased to be separate beings as they soared away together to some lofty place of bliss and delight.

Just when it became too wonderful to bear, the soft explosion of *more,* both splintered her into pieces then brought her back together, forever changed. Too soon, they fell toward earth, landing in each other's arms in the darkened room.

Claire lay beneath him trembling as what they'd done gradually began to impact her. As mistakes went, it was a doozy, but the wonder of it wrapped her in a gauzy cocoon

of rightness. The runaway train that mas-
queraded as their marriage had just rocketed
into another distant station.

They'd consummated their marriage, but
their relationship was less than a week old.
The feeling that her life was again going
completely out of control caused a small,
quick panic, and the fact that *she'd* just gone
so completely out of control gave her another
fleeting taste of panic.

Her chaste life was well and truly gone,
and the man she'd given her chastity to
hadn't said a single word that even hinted at
love. That was the panic that showed up next,
but that was the one that lingered.

Then she remembered that she'd been anything but silent. Had she truly said, ''I love
you'' to Logan? More than once? Oh, surely
not! The fact that she couldn't be certain
brought a cold trickle of worry.

Ironically, from Logan's point of view, it
apparently hadn't been too soon for him to
seduce her, but she knew right away that it

had been too soon for her to confess love to him. He either wouldn't believe her, or he'd feel pressured to confess some sort of affection for her.

And of course he wouldn't do that. The man who'd told her love wasn't a requirement was a man too cynical to believe in the possibility that either of them could feel it this soon, in spite of whatever spectacular sexual thing had just happened between them.

Claire tried not to be disturbed by the silence between them as they lay in the dark bedroom. Eventually, the heavy drowsiness that gripped her body smothered her worries and she slept deeply.

He'd had the bad luck to marry a woman who was too emotional and expressive to keep her emotions and expressions to herself. Logan had known that already, and he should have been prepared for a sexual novice to come out with unguarded words in the heat of passion.

A woman more jaded by experience would never have said them, but Claire was anything but jaded. Still, he would have bet money that pride alone would keep her from making that kind of declaration.

On second thought, a woman who'd never given herself to a man might need to convince herself that she was in love before she allowed sex. Claire had been persnickety longer than most, so it made sense that she might confuse what her body felt for love.

His conscience calmed a little at the idea. And anyway, hadn't he decided it was all right for her to love him as long as she didn't expect him to feel the same for her?

If there was one thing he'd learned about Claire, it was that she was generous with her affection. Cody was the prime recipient of that generosity, but she'd evidently decided her husband was deserving of it, too.

A woman like Claire would be generous with everyone, so her generosity in raising her stepsister's son and then giving him and this marriage a fair chance wasn't that unusual for her or especially significant. She'd likely allowed sex tonight because it fit with her notion of a marriage commitment. And since a woman like her wouldn't have sex without feeling love first, she'd needed to believe she was in love whether she really was or not.

Relieved to see that, Logan pulled her a little more snugly against him, enjoying the sweetness of her warm, satiny skin against his.

The tenderness he felt for her now troubled him. Though it wasn't love—it could never be love—he'd need to be on his guard. Claire was more exciting than he'd expected, much more. It was safe to like her, safe to be fond of her, but love gave a woman too much power, particularly one as bright as Claire. Years before he'd chosen her, he'd made up his mind not to succumb to that kind of foolishness. It hadn't taken long last Thursday to realize that a woman like her could twist him up like a pretzel if she even half tried. But only if he was crazy enough to fall for her.

Certain he was immune to whatever manipulation his clever and bewitching little wife might want to try on him, Logan closed his eyes. But he couldn't sleep.

Claire was grateful to wake up before Logan and make it to the sanctuary of the bathroom before he opened his eyes. Though they'd been intimate, she felt uncharacteristically shy about facing him that morning.

Other than a mouth that looked as if it had been kissed, there was no sign that she was any different on the outside. Inside, she felt warm and prickly, and her body was yearning for more of the things that she couldn't have imagined this time yesterday.

She'd considered herself well-informed, but nothing could have truly prepared her for what it had been like last night when Logan had made love to her.

Made love? Her heart sank a little. She was well aware that a man could have sex without involving his heart, but she wasn't wired that way. Surely Logan couldn't stay married to her and not allow himself to love her at some point if he at least liked her now. For all his apparent cynicism, he'd have to be as heartless as she'd first taken him to be if he couldn't eventually develop strong feelings for a wife he lived with day in and day out.

Particularly when the wife he'd slept with last night wasn't on the pill. A wife who, judging by the calendar, just might have conceived his child last night.

A worry she'd never had and had never imagined having, given her conservative lifestyle, began to pick at her. It amazed her that she'd not given a single thought to birth control last night. Logan hadn't seemed to give birth control a thought either, but now that she was remembering his mention of children, she doubted very much that he'd planned to do anything about it, even if she brought up the subject.

Well, there was no way she wanted to rocket into yet another distant train station, particularly not *that* one. And she'd never want to if Logan didn't—or proved he couldn't—love her.

Rattled, Claire finished in the bathroom and got dressed, then slipped out of the bathroom to rush to the kitchen to put on the coffee. When she finished, she stood over the sink, gripping the edge of the counter as she debated whether to mention the birth control problem. Her more immediate worry was what to say and how to behave when she finally had to face Logan.

In the end, she needn't have worried. The minute she saw Logan's stony expression and sensed his aloofness, she knew it was better to stay silent and match that aloofness. At least until she could think of a way to breach the uneasy distance between them.

CHAPTER ELEVEN

THE closer they got to Pierce Ranch, the lower Claire's spirits sagged. Logan was largely uncommunicative, so she was too.

Could there be something else on his mind, or was this truly about three little words, spoken while she was half out of her mind with pleasure? Claire couldn't imagine what else accounted for Logan's behavior that day, and she knew it was only a matter of time before she'd have to know for sure.

But then she thought of something else that made her worries over Logan's silence worse, and she felt her feminine pride take a hefty punch. Logan was sexually experienced, but she was not. Could his silence be because he'd been disappointed by her... performance? Had making love to her been unsatisfying for him?

It was true that she'd been so caught up in what was happening to her that she'd been distracted. He'd seemed plenty satisfied at the time, but then, there might be degrees of satisfaction. In her mind, she'd been wildly passionate and shamelessly eager, responding to him just the way she should have—mostly because she couldn't have stopped herself—but what if she'd somehow not measured up?

Then again, he'd seemed to appreciate that she'd been a virgin, so he had to know to expect more enthusiasm than…

She couldn't think of a word similar to the word "skill," which sounded a bit too professional for comfort. But was that the problem? Had she disappointed him so much that he didn't think things would get better?

Because she was the kind of person who prided herself in doing things properly and correctly and well, the idea of not measuring up in something so important was hard on her ego.

It was a relief to finally reach the ranch, if for no other reason than the fact that some of the tension between them was burned off getting her things into the house. Logan called a couple of his men to help, and the task was finished in no time.

Logan left Cody with Claire while he took the one-way rental trailer into town to turn it in to the local office. Claire welcomed the time he was gone, and she quickly unpacked the boxes she'd had the ranch hands carry into the master bedroom.

Everything else had been put in one of the guest rooms, so there was no rush with those. While she worked, Cody played on some of the unopened boxes until she was ready to deal with them. Afterward, he played with the empty boxes, stacking them like blocks or dragging them around.

When Claire finished, she helped him stack them four high then watched as he tumbled them over, surveyed the result, then set about restacking them for another fall. Claire sat

down on the bed to watch, taking what enjoyment she could from watching him play
until he tired of it and abandoned the boxes
to go back to his bedroom and the rocking
horse.

Claire walked out to the hall then into the
main part of the house, but Logan hadn't returned from town yet. Since it was almost
time for lunch, she went back to get Cody
changed and washed up. Logan still hadn't
returned by the time they'd sat down to
lunch, and Claire's appetite was just as absent
as he was.

Those next days were a huge disappointment.
Logan did indeed spend almost every day-
light hour outdoors, as remote as ever. The
only times they did anything as a family were
at meals and after supper when they all went
down to the corrals to let Cody ride the pony.

There'd been no further riding instruction
for Claire. It was as if Logan had changed
his mind about that, and she couldn't take it

as anything but another negative. Nothing was said about when they'd begin adoption proceedings, and Claire wasn't ready to ask until Logan was more approachable on any subject.

The only time things were different between them was in bed. It was there that Logan warmed up, but it was also there that Claire promptly gave him enough of an icy response to keep him on his side of the mattress. How dare he?

If he was going to behave like a coldhearted cretin during the day, he could darned well continue being one once the lights were off. He was getting her message loud and clear, but he was too stubborn to acknowledge it, much less offer to talk things over with her.

At first, Claire had decided he'd have to be the one to change things, since he'd been the one who'd instigated everything, from their marriage to their one night of intimacy. She'd credited them both with more maturity than this silent standoff, but she felt hurt enough to keep her own childish distance.

At least Logan made time for Cody. Every night with the pony, but afterwards with the little boy in the den, playing with the old toys. Claire kept out of that, because it was important for Logan to forge his own relationship with his nephew, since that relationship was the most important, whatever happened between her and Logan.

By Monday, Claire had decided enough was enough, that she couldn't stand another moment of silence. To keep herself from going to find Logan and having it out right then, she took Cody into town after his nap that afternoon to have a look around and see about buying the sturdy clothes that Logan had mentioned their first night on the ranch. She'd rather have dragged him along to get his input, but she was leery of getting a "too busy" excuse.

She didn't trust herself not to immediately confront him if he did that. And though she was itching for a showdown, this wasn't the time to try. Maybe once she cooled off, but she also needed to see some sign that Logan might be open to talking first, or they might get into an all out war.

They'd just looked through the first couple of shops that sold western wear when Kiki Lynch stopped them on the sidewalk.

''Bored with ranch life already?'' she asked, and Claire couldn't miss the mocking curl to one corner of the beautiful brunette's mouth.

Claire smiled as if she was oblivious to the small jab. ''Just out having a look around while Logan's busy.

''By the way,'' she added, suddenly inspired. ''Since you're a horsewoman, could you give me some advice? Logan mentioned that Cody and I needed hats and boots and sturdy clothes, but I couldn't decide what to pick. The jeans seemed awfully stiff, and there must be a jillion kinds of hats and a half dozen kinds of boot heels. Can I rely on the shop people to know what I need or should I find someone like you to advise me?''

Claire had just that moment decided that if she was going to make a life with Logan—assuming their marriage wasn't already on the rocks—she'd need to live at peace with everyone, at least with the people Logan knew and interacted with. Right now, Kiki Lynch was the only one she'd met so far, and a little diplomacy might overcome at least a bit of the woman's obvious hostility.

Plus, there was also the possibility that Kiki might mention something that would give her a clue to her enigmatic husband. Even if Kiki gave misinformation, Claire might at least be able to get an inkling of something.

Kiki showed only a small spark of surprise before she smiled. Claire didn't quite trust that smile, but she remained hopeful.

''Well, sure I could, Carla. How 'bout now?''

"Now would be wonderful. I'd really appreciate it, but I only have an hour or so before we have to head back for supper."

"Ah, it shouldn't take long," Kiki told her, and the woman looked as if she was warming to the idea more by the moment. "We females know how to pull into the fast lane when we have to, don't we?"

Claire made herself give a light laugh. "That's why we use credit cards, isn't it? So we can say, 'Charge!'?"

Kiki laughed at that little chestnut and for the tiniest moment, Claire saw a trace of honest amusement.

But then the whirlwind shopping spree Kiki had decided on caught them both up. Cody went along, innocently unaware that his mommy was giving her private credit cards the workout of their lives. Always one to pay off her credit balances each month, Claire had to grit her teeth to comply with each of Kiki's notions of what she and Cody couldn't live without.

She pictured her small savings account dwindling by the second, but she complied with everything Kiki suggested. After all, she could always bring things back later if some turned out to be unwise purchases. The important thing was to give Kiki the opportunity to be a friend rather than a foe.

And also to see if she'd spill the beans about something. In the end though, the only thing that got spilled was Claire's rigid notions about prudent spending. She'd never spent so much at one time for clothes in her life, for either her or Cody!

By the time Kiki helped her carry everything to her car, there were enough bags and boxes to bury the back seat. Cody was already wearing his new boots and hat, stomping around on any kind of floor covering in the shops as well as on the sidewalk to listen to the sound they made.

Before Claire could become too effusive with her thanks to Kiki, she found herself agreeing to be at the Lynch ranch in the morning for riding lessons.

Kiki's laughing, "You want to learn to ride with a little female elegance, Carla," sounded like the biggest booby trap of all time, but Kiki had clearly decided to take Claire under her wing. Whether Kiki meant to help her or not remained to be seen, unless Claire could think of a good excuse to cancel it or put it off.

Though Claire had expected Kiki to have her buy things that were completely out of line, she didn't seem to have done that. In fact, it was Claire who'd fallen in love with the red Western boots she'd bought to wear for special occasions. Kiki had strongly advised her to buy black ones for regular days on the ranch, but Claire hadn't been able to resist adding the flashy red ones, and her credit cards were swooning from the shock.

Once she and Cody were in the car and they'd reached the highway just outside town, Claire absently glanced at the clock on the dash and felt a jolt. They were late, late, *late* for supper!

Claire had got so caught up in the shopping spree that instead of the hour she'd thought had passed, it had been closer to two hours. Logan hadn't been around when she'd decided to go so he hadn't known about this, though Elsa did.

Claire hadn't given a thought to calling the ranch before they'd left town because she hadn't paid attention to the time. Now that they were on the highway, it would delay them even more if she drove back to find a pay phone, so she kept going. It hadn't occurred to her to ask Elsa if Logan had a cell phone that she could take along, but she sorely wished now that she had.

When she and Cody finally arrived at the ranch and got out, she let the boy carry two of the shopping bags while she gathered up as many handles as she could and followed him. He got to the door before her, but set his bags down, then promptly kicked the toe of his boots against one of the bags to listen to the paper rattle. The big front door abruptly swung open just as Claire stepped in behind Cody.

Logan's expression was deathly harsh, and his dark eyes glittered with temper. Claire made herself give him a chastened smile.

"I'm sorry we're late. We were trying to get the clothes you'd mentioned, and time got completely away from me. I hope Elsa wasn't inconvenienced by my thoughtlessness. Or you," she added.

It was discourteous to be late without letting anyone know first, and she genuinely did regret the inconvenience. And she knew already that being this late wouldn't win her gold stars with her touchy and still remote husband.

"Is the rest in the car?" he asked gruffly.

"Well, yes. Both boxes and more shopping bags. I can get them myself once I put these things inside."

"I'll get 'em," he growled, and Claire moved a little out of the way as he stepped past Cody to stalk to the car. She glanced back as he went, then herded Cody inside with their things.

She had a few moments, so she rushed through the house with their things to put them in the hall next to their bedrooms to be sorted and divided up later, then sprinted back to arrive at the door just in time for Logan to walk in with their boot and hat boxes, and the handles of four shopping bags that dangled two each from his little fingers.

He set the stack on the table in the foyer, stood the bags out of the way on the floor, and Claire closed the front door. Cody was clomping around on the tile still wearing his new kid-sized cowboy hat, and Logan turned to watch. His stony face cracked a little and he looked over at Claire.

"Those look good. And he must like the sound of new boots."

It was an unexpected reprieve. Almost as if in spite of his ire over their lateness, Logan was now extending an olive branch.

''He stomped over half of town to try them out. And I'll bet you'll have a hard time getting him to take off the hat. He said he wanted one like *Unco's,* so it had to be black. I couldn't tell, but I have it on good authority that it's exactly like yours.''

Now his stony expression relented a little more. ''Whose authority?''

''Kiki's. Actually, she helped us pick out the things she thought you'd want. Or at least, most of the things. It was so generous of her to do that, but—'' Claire hesitated. ''Remember when you see the red boots that those were my idea, not hers.''

''You didn't buy red boots for the boy, did you?'' The idea clearly wasn't one that pleased him.

''Oh, no,'' she said quickly, lacing her fingers together in front of her. ''They're mine.

But Kiki advised me to stick with the black ones for everyday, which I also bought.''

He gave her a narrow look. ''I haven't given you a set of credit cards yet.''

''I have my own cards and bank account.'' Claire winced playfully. ''Or rather, I will until the end of the month when the bills come due.''

Logan looked as if he'd have more to say on this later, but he turned his attention back to Cody. ''Supper's sitting in the oven, so we'd better eat.''

Claire sensed that the small storm she'd created had completely calmed, and she hurried Cody into the hall bathroom to get his hands washed before she left him in the dining room with Logan and went to get their supper out of the oven. So far so good.

After a fairly pleasant supper, Claire cleared the table, loaded the dishwasher and started it before they all went down to the corrals. When Cody's ride was finished for the night, he and Claire showed Logan their new things, and Claire was relieved that it all passed muster. Including her red boots.

Cody was tired enough to go to bed a little early. Once they finished with what had become a nighttime routine for all of them, Claire lingered near Cody's room until she was sure he'd settled before she went in search of Logan.

Perhaps the fact that he'd backed down on the issue of her being so late was a signal that things were improving between them. She'd been hoping for some sign that he might be ready to talk things out, and this might be the best opportunity that would come along. Since she couldn't stand things the way they were, she had to make the most of this.

To her surprise, Logan was merely sitting at his desk with his chair turned so he was facing one of the bookcases. The desk blotter was clear of papers, the computer screen was turned off, and he looked as if he was brooding over something that troubled him.

Claire rapped her knuckles lightly on the door frame, rewarded when he glanced over at her. There was none of the cool aloofness she'd seen so much of, but she sensed his wariness. At least she could see that much difference, and it gave her hope.

She crossed the room, but having the desk between them seemed too formal, so she walked around to his side and half sat on the edge of the desk beside his chair arm, as if she meant to have a friendly chat.

She'd been intimate with this man almost a week ago, so she needed to reclaim a small bit of that intimacy and make it verbal. She laced her fingers together and rested them on her slanted lap before she began.

"I appreciate that you understood about us being late," she said, then gave him what she hoped was a more intent look so he'd get the message. "I can only imagine what you thought."

His voice was low and rough. "Don't make a habit of it." He'd missed her hint, so she repeated it softly.

"I can only imagine what you thought."

He caught it this time and leaned back in his big chair to study her face. She dared more.

"I can only imagine what you thought, because all I'll ever have is what I can imagine if we can't talk so I can be sure." She kept her gaze steady on his. "And I think you do some imagining of your own. Yes, you might have hired an investigator, and you might have found out a few more things about me by experience this past week and a half, but there's still too much room for your imagination to work overtime, just like mine is now. And, without the facts, I think both our imaginations will lead us seriously wrong. Considering what I've been going through with mine, I sincerely hope so."

His dark gaze fell away from hers, but not before she caught a hint of frustration and regret.

"Claire..." His voice was a growl, and because he hesitated a moment, she rushed in.

"Tell me what I did wrong, Logan, please. Was it what I said, or did I just not…satisfy you?"

That got her his immediate attention and she saw the horror on his face. "No. *Hell* no, honey." He shook his head then gave a rueful chuckle that did wonders for her ego. "It was the best I—" Logan cut off that comment to switch to, "Let's just say I was satisfied, Claire. Don't let your *imagination* tell you different."

"Then, was it because I told you I love you?" Her soft, quick words dropped neatly into the discussion.

It was amazing how quickly Logan's expression went somber and hard. Claire didn't want to lose this opportunity, so she reached out to put her hand over the top of his as it rested on the chair arm. She was compelled to be direct with him.

"I think I deserve to hear why you told me you don't require love in this marriage."

That made his stoniness falter and he glanced uneasily away with another gruff, "Claire..."

"If you refuse to love me, then it might be some small comfort to know why you won't. And I hope it's a really strong reason, one I can understand and try to accept. Because it's not just my happiness that will be affected, but yours too. And Cody's."

"It's old history," he growled again.

Claire gave his hand a gentle squeeze. "I don't doubt that," she agreed, "but I don't want to pay for old history that had nothing to do with what I've done or will do in the future. Don't I qualify for a chance of my own with you?"

He growled again and abruptly snatched her off the edge of the desk to his lap as if she were no bigger than Cody. He held her with one arm and caught the back of her head with his hand to pull her close for a fiery kiss.

She tasted his anger and his frustration, but he immediately gentled the kiss then dragged his lips away to cinch her tightly against him with hard, strong arms. Claire's cheek rested near his throat and her forehead was pressed against his jaw.

The moments pulsed by and she kept utterly silent and still, hoping he'd speak and expose the mysteries. She could feel the small war in him, but then it began to calm and she was afraid he'd decided not to tell her.

"My mother was a piece of work," he said at last. "She looked fragile, but she was stronger than most men who do hard labor. My daddy was crazy about her, but the only thing she seemed to love about him was his money."

Claire all but held her breath as she listened.

"She hated the ranch, so she tried to live in town or travel as much as possible. When Daddy put his foot down, she got even by going to work on Cliff and me, filling our heads with nonsense.

''She wanted us to hate this place as much as she did, and she wanted us to take her side against Daddy. It didn't work on me, but Cliff was a lot younger so she had a lot more influence on him. And yet it didn't matter to our daddy what she did to him or what she did to us, or even how many times she betrayed him by trying to turn us against him. He knew about it, but he was so crazy about her that all he did was make up excuses about why she did it.''

He stopped for a while as if lost in memory. If he didn't go on, he'd given her enough information to understand a lot of things. Now she knew why he'd warned her about coming between him and Cody, and about spoiling Cody on the ranch.

Another message was also coming through loud and clear: Logan believed that it had been his father's love for his mother that had set him up and made him vulnerable to being manipulated and used and betrayed, and for

them all to be set up for turmoil and unhap-
piness.

"She played on his feelings for her," he
said, "time after time, working him, accusing
him of not loving her, going around teary-
eyed and refusing to eat."

He paused briefly then said, "I'm glad he
outlived her. At least she didn't get control
of this place. If she had, she would have sold
it to the first buyer who came along. She had
no respect for anything to do with this ranch
except for the income it and the oil wells gen-
erated. My daddy never got over her, and
died loving her. He didn't last two years after
she was killed...crossing the street in San
Antonio."

He chuckled then, but it sounded weary
and cynical and anything but truly amused.
"How's that for irony?"

Claire's fingers had been toying absently
with one of the buttons on his shirt as she'd
concentrated on every word he'd said, but
now she flattened her palm on his chest. "I'm

sorry, Logan. What a confusing way to grow up.''

She lifted her head and looked into his face. ''I'm glad you told me. But there's something else I'd like to know.''

Logan moved his hand and brushed the back of a knuckle against her cheek. ''I think I can guess,'' he said, then smiled faintly.

Claire could see the dark memories that still lingered in his eyes, and she suddenly knew that the whole story about his parents was uglier than he'd let on, but she could tell just by the fact that he'd told her as much as he had that he was already letting some of it go.

She smiled softly back. ''All right. Let's see how good a guesser you are.'' He started right away.

''You want to know if I'll give you a chance to be you, and if you'll have to pay for my momma's mistakes. *And* my daddy's.''

Claire leaned back from him a little, still searching his dark eyes and every nuance of his somber expression before she confirmed his guesses.

"I don't expect instant trust," she said, "and I don't expect you to force yourself to feel something for me that you don't. I just don't want you to refuse the possibility, or to refuse to let it happen. *If* it happens."

She'd added that last to protect her pride, though she didn't know why. It would probably hurt her pride more if he honestly couldn't love her than if he simply refused to love her.

Logan's callused fingertips traced lightly along her cheek. "*If,* huh? I thought you were more perceptive than that, Claire."

Now he gave her that slow, sexy smile that made him so breathtakingly handsome. All at once she knew that Logan had passed some personal milestone, that they both had. But common sense told her she already loved him too much to chance letting her hopes get too high about what might happen next.

And it was too soon especially to believe that she'd just heard him give a significant hint about what might happen next. Or about what he might confess, though her heart was fluttering with excitement.

"No, it's not what *I* mean by saying 'If,'" she ventured, a little breathless, "it's what do *you* mean by saying 'If'?"

Now his smile widened. "*If,* Claire? *If* it happens? You don't miss much, honey, so I can't figure how you'd miss what the past few days have been about."

Claire lifted her brows at that. "Far be it from me to presume," she lied, then had to deal with a nervous giggle that almost got free as she felt her heart begin to rise with wild hope.

"All right," he said, "I'm prepared to indulge my wife. The past few days have really been about the fact that there was never any '*If* it happens.' Mainly because '*It*' had already happened, and I knew it as far back as when you stood in the hall outside the living room that first day and glared up at me like a she-cat. You practically growled when you told me Cody wasn't a week old or a month old, that he was a trusting little boy who'd lived all his life with his momma. You were dying to call me the most wicked, dastardly monster on the planet, because you loved a kid you were terrified I wouldn't treat right. That's when *'It'* happened—even though I refused to believe it.''

Claire felt a flush go through her from head to toe. ''It?''

Logan leaned his head back as if she'd worn him out. ''Please, darlin'. First it's *'if,'* and now it's *'it.'* Let's just do the shorthand and call it *'love.'*'' He lifted his head and pulled her closer. ''I love you, Claire. I can't stand going on like we have for the past week, so how 'bout we just say the words then go prove it to each other all night?''

It was Claire who put her palm on his lean cheek then kissed him, softly, sweetly, so emotional about it that her eyes stung. She drew back only long enough to say, ''I love you,'' before she kissed him again.

Sometime in between that next handful of kisses, Logan breathed the words, ''I love you, Claire,'' at least twice.

And then he gathered her up and rolled back the desk chair to stand. As he carried her to the bedroom end of the house, they kissed their way there, turning off lights, then pausing as they kissed some more.

Claire's heart was still pounding with the wonder of it, but any worries she'd had about their sudden marriage and the future began to melt away with each gentle love word and assurance.

Later, after they'd truly consummated their love, they lay together in the dim light Logan had left on, talking. Eventually the talk meandered to Kiki's invitation for that next morning.

Logan laughed when she told him, then went grim and ground out a low, "There's not a single way on God's green earth that I'll let Kiki Lynch give *my* wife riding lessons."

Claire smiled at that. She already knew he was right. "She told me that I would want to learn to ride with a little 'female elegance.' But then she called me Carla again, and I knew she might still have a teensy bit of animosity toward me. I was hoping I could tell her that you were taking me riding in the morning so I could get out of it politely. After all, she was very good to shop with me for the right clothes today. I don't want to hurt her feelings or offend her."

Logan rose up on an elbow to give her a suspicious look that was pure playacting. "Is that why we had our talk earlier? Because you wanted me to get you out of going to Kiki's tomorrow?"

Claire rolled her eyes. "Oh my, will I have to prove my sincerity to you *again* tonight?"

Logan gave her a broad grin and leaned down. ''I was hopin' you would, darlin','' he rasped. ''And then maybe again after that,'' he added as his lips covered hers.

There was nothing more for a while but the sounds and tender acts of a man and a woman who were delighted with each other and passionate about it.

A man and a woman who would soon grow to be too devoted to each other and too much in love to do anything less than succeed with the marriage and the life they'd build for themselves. A marriage and a life they'd build and share, not only with each other and the sweet child they had now, but also with the sweet children who would come later.

MILLS & BOON® PUBLISH EIGHT LARGE PRINT TITLES A MONTH. THESE ARE THE EIGHT TITLES FOR MARCH 2004

THE ITALIAN BOSS'S MISTRESS
Lynne Graham

THE BEDROOM SURRENDER
Emma Darcy

A SPANISH VENGEANCE
Diana Hamilton

THE MILLIONAIRE'S VIRGIN MISTRESS
Robyn Donald

THE ACCIDENTAL MISTRESS
Sophie Weston

THE BRIDE ASSIGNMENT
Leigh Michaels

THE MARRIAGE COMMAND
Susan Fox

A SURPRISE CHRISTMAS PROPOSAL
Liz Fielding

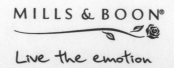

MILLS & BOON®

Live the emotion

0204 Rom LP

MILLS & BOON® PUBLISH EIGHT LARGE PRINT TITLES A MONTH. THESE ARE THE EIGHT TITLES FOR APRIL 2004

THE SALVATORE MARRIAGE
Michelle Reid

THE CHRISTMAS MARRIAGE MISSION
Helen Brooks

THE SPANIARD'S PASSION
Jane Porter

THE YULETIDE ENGAGEMENT
Carole Mortimer

OUTBACK SURRENDER
Margaret Way

THE ITALIAN'S BABY
Lucy Gordon

THE WEDDING WISH
Ally Blake

A BRIDE FOR THE HOLIDAYS
Renee Roszel

MILLS & BOON®

Live the emotion

0304 Rom LP